Annie's life is full. The last thing she needs is a serious relationship. . .

"Do you do a lot of dating?" he asked her abruptly.

Annie laughed softly. She couldn't help it. "I knew you were going to ask something like that."

Dan looked both embarrassed and relieved by her admission. "I hope I haven't insulted or offended you by asking that question. Believe me, that's not my intent. And you don't have to answer it, either. I'm just wondering what kind of a woman you are. . .or were before you got saved. And, not to judge you, Annie, but just to. . .to get to know you better." He frowned. "Am I making sense? I don't feel like I am."

"Back on the farm, we called that 'hoof-in-mouth disease'," Annie teased him.

Dan chuckled, looking chagrined. "Touché. I guess I have stuck my foot in my mouth."

"Well, to answer your question, Dan, and, yes, I'll answer it. . .I'm not offended, either. But, no, I don't do a lot of dating," she said in her most serious tone of voice. Annie had a point to make, and the sooner she made it the better. For both of them. The last thing she needed or wanted in her life was another person to worry about. Another mouth to feed. Another human being to take care of? No way! "I don't date at all, in fact," she continued, "so please don't ask me out because I'll just turn you down."

ANDREA BOESHAAR, who also writes as Andrea Shaar, makes her home in Wisconsin. Her writings reflect her conviction that God is always in control.

HEARTSONG PRESENTS

Books by Andrea Shaar
HP79—An Unwilling Warrior

Books by Andrea Boeshaar
HP188—An Uncertain Heart

Annie's Song

Andrea Boeshaar

Heartsong Presents

*The idea for this story began when
my husband, Daniel, said, "You know,
I always wanted to play the piano. . ."*

To Daniel with love

A note from the Author:
*I love to hear from my readers! You may write to me at
the following address:*   **Andrea Boeshaar**
                            Author Relations
                            P.O. Box 719
                            Uhrichsville, OH 44683

ISBN 1-57748-153-4

ANNIE'S SONG

Cover design by Robyn Martins.

PRINTED IN THE U.S.A.

one

Annie Fetherston's fingers danced across the keys of the cash register—$5.72 for the chicken, $ .79 for the eggs, $ .89 for the toilet paper, $1.19 for the potatoes. . .

"Think you'd like to get another ten pounds?" Annie asked the customer as she hit the subtotal button. "The potatoes are on sale this week."

The woman's brows went up in surprise. Then she nodded, and Annie watched as she made her way across the green and white linoleum, heading for the produce aisle. The customer looked like a harried housewife, complete with rollers in her hair and a kerchief around her head. Annie smiled. She knew and understood the feeling well—there weren't enough hours in the day to wash and set your hair and get the grocery shopping done.

The woman came back with the potatoes and, pulling out two brown paper bags from beneath the checkout counter, Annie began to pack up the groceries. With that completed, she gave the woman her total, took the ten dollar bill, made change, and wished her a good evening.

"That's it for the day, Annie," John Winston, the owner, said as he locked the plate glass door. "Ring out."

"Sure thing," Annie replied with a smile. Then she turned the key in the cash register, punched in her code, and let the machine do its thing.

John came up behind her. "Technology," he said in a tone of amusement that bordered on sarcasm. "Where would we be without it?"

Annie continued to smile. "We'd be here till seven tonight counting our coins, that's where we'd be!"

She laughed along with John, who moved on to the office cubicle on the other side of the four checkout lanes. Then, folding her arms, Annie leaned back against the counter and waited for her machine to ring out. She yawned and glanced at her wristwatch: three minutes past five o'clock.

Today had been a long, busy one. The store opened at seven o'clock every morning except for Sunday, when it was closed altogether. Today being Saturday, it had opened at 7:00 A.M. on the button. Annie had worked the nine-to-five shift while Candy, another checker, had worked eight to four, and Maggy, John's wife and co-owner, had worked seven to three. Only three checkers, but sometimes John opened a lane if the place was crowded. Most times, though, three were enough.

Paradigm Foods was a small grocery store and one of the few left that was locally owned. Bigger, faster, busier food-store chains had moved into this small, northern town of Rhinelander, Wisconsin, mostly to accommodate the tourist population. Fall brought the deer hunters; winter, the snowmo-bilers and skiers; and summer brought the lake cottage people and the artists who attended the School of the Arts. Residents complained that they couldn't tell anymore who was local folk and who wasn't. However, Annie could usually spot a tourist a mile away. It was the expression in his eyes. . .that look of total confusion. Or driving the wrong way on a one-way street. Of course, Annie had to admit, she knew some locals who did that, too!

Tearing off a long slip of white paper produced by the cash register, Annie collected her drawer of money and pouch of coupons and walked over to the office where John was clos-ing up shop. He was a good guy in Annie's opinion, and he seemed like a devoted husband and father. He was a good boss, for sure—Annie hadn't ever had one better. John and Maggy took care of her—even providing her with health insurance for herself and her two sons and free near-to-expiration-date perishables in the store like bread, milk, produce, and meats. Sometimes Annie wondered how John and Maggy Winston could even afford to keep their doors open.

"So," John began, "Maggy told me that you're coming to our church's Friend Day tomorrow."

Annie grimaced. She was hoping Maggy hadn't said any-thing to John—or, if she had, that he would have forgotten! No such luck, it would seem.

"Are your boys coming, too?" John asked, taking her drawer

and locking it in the safe. "They're invited, too, you know."

"Uhm. . .well. . ."

"They're older than our kids, aren't they? Maggy said your oldest is sixteen."

Annie nodded. "Stephen." She didn't talk about him much. He was her "problem child."

"And the other one is Josh, right?"

Again Annie nodded. "He's twelve. You've met him a couple of times when he's come into the store."

"Of course."

"I don't think my boys will come."

"Well, don't worry if they won't," John told her. "Just get yourself there. I know Maggy will be really disappointed if you don't show up."

Annie grimaced for the second time. She wasn't a church-going person, but she didn't want to disappoint Maggy, either. The woman had been good to Annie this past year—ever since Annie began working at Paradigm Foods. Maggy had listened to those few times when Annie had divulged her problems concerning her boys. As a single mother for the last five and a half years—ever since her husband, Eric, had died—raising two sons had been a heartache for Annie rather than the joy of motherhood!

"What time is that church service again?" Annie asked almost reluctantly.

"Ten-thirty," John replied with a broad grin. "Oh, and Maggy said she'll wait for you out in the foyer of the church."

Forcing a little smile, Annie nodded. "Okay. Well, I guess I'll see you tomorrow, then."

John smacked the desktop with his palm. "Good!" he exclaimed with a grand smile. "It'll be great. You'll love it."

Annie gave him a curious look, wondering how a man could get so excited over a church service.

"Well, see you tomorrow," she said again, grabbing her purse and sweater before leaving the store.

It was early October, and the weather was cool but pleasant. It had been a warm, sunny day; however, as the sun went down, so did the temperature.

Walking down Lincoln Street, Annie inhaled. It felt good to

be outside, filling her lungs with fresh air. The best part of a workday, she decided, was getting to the end of it! There was something rewarding about finishing up a job well done and something relaxing about the "eventide," as Annie's father used to call it.

Work was nothing new to Annie Fetherston. She'd grown up on a farm and helped with the livestock and crops. Then she quit high school at the age of seventeen so she could take care of her mother who had cancer. Annie's mother died two years later—just before Annie met Eric Fetherston. Six months after that, they were married.

Eric had been a truck driver, and Annie had been a full-time wife. . .until Stephen was born. Then she was a full-time wife and a full-time mother. Josh, Annie's youngest, was born four years later, and they should have been—could have been—a cozy, happy family except for the fact that Eric wasn't all that interested in being a husband and father. He had had his job, his friends, and his hobbies: baseball, bowling, playing cards, deer hunting. And trucking kept him on the road and away from home. Eric, it seemed, had always been away doing something while Annie stayed home and did those things that were part of her "job"—ironing, scrubbing, changing diapers, and doing laundry.

But one day Eric's truck hit a patch of ice and overturned on the interstate, killing Eric. Annie had been forced to get a job—a real job, as Eric used to call working outside the home. He hadn't had much respect for homemakers, even though he enjoyed the way Annie took care of him and their children—and Eric always seemed to require the most care. He had been kind of a high-maintenance person in Annie's opinion. But she had loved him, and though it had been years since his death, she still missed him sometimes. She missed being part of a whole—a couple. Except she sure didn't need another person to take care of! She had enough to manage with her responsibilities still waiting for her at home and now having to work at a real job, too!

But one day. . .one day when her boys were grown and gone, Annie dreamed of going back to school. She wanted to make something of herself. She wanted a. . .a purpose.

Something at which she could succeed, since most of her life seemed bland, even bleak.

Turning the corner onto Eastern Avenue, Annie paused, her daydreams tossed aside. She could hear it even from the corner. Stephen had his rock and roll blaring, and Annie feared the neighbors would complain again!

She hurried down the sidewalk, which was bubbled and cracked in several places. "Oh, Stephen," she mumbled under her breath, "how many times have I told you not to play your music so loud? I've told you a hundred times if I told you once."

Annie was still muttering as she entered the side door of her small, wood-framed house. It was painted a pale yellow with white trim around the two stories of windows, and though it needed much work, it was still home.

"Stephen!" she called as she set her purse on the kitchen table. Then she realized how ridiculous it was—he couldn't hear her calling over that loud, horrible stuff!

Holding her ears, Annie climbed the carpeted stairs, avoiding the worn spots, lest she make them worse. Then, at Stephen's bedroom, she knocked. When there was no reply, she pushed the door open.

"Mom!" Stephen said in surprise. He quickly jumped up from where he'd been sitting on the bed and turned down his stereo. Two strange-looking young men, each in blue jeans and an oversized shirt, sat on the other twin bed, across from where Stephen had been. One of the boys had chin-length brown hair and a hoop earring. The other had a spiked haircut that had been dyed pink at the top. "We're just hanging out, Mom," Stephen explained.

Annie forced a smile. She thought she smelled cigarette smoke, but she couldn't be sure since Stephen had the window open. She also thought she smelled air freshener. Or was that somebody's cologne?

"I don't think I've met your. . .your friends, Stephen," Annie said pointedly.

"Oh, yeah." He cleared his throat and then all three boys started laughing as if it were some great joke that a mother wanted to know who her son was hanging out with. "Well, like, this is Ed Johnson," Stephen said of the boy with the earring. "And this is Pete Cunningham."

"Nice to meet you," Annie said warily, nodding at each of them. "And now, Stephen, I'd like a word with you, please."

He shrugged. "Sure."

Annie escorted him downstairs to the kitchen.

"Were you smoking cigarettes up there?" she asked sternly.

"Cigarettes?" Stephen exaggerated a surprised look. Then he combed strong, young fingers through his thick, wavy, black hair that was nearly to his shoulders. "Not cigarettes, Mom. Us?" He laughed. "C'mon, Mom. We're good boys."

Annie narrowed her gaze. "Yeah, sure you are."

Ed and Pete suddenly burst into the kitchen. "See ya, Mrs. Fetherston," they said, one right after the other. Then Pink Top Pete, as Annie immediately dubbed him, added, "Hurry up, Steve, we'll be out in the car." Moments later, they were both out the side door and gone.

"The car?" Annie's heart did a leap into her throat. "Oh no! You're not climbing into a car with those guys! I have no idea who they are or. . .or what planet they're from!"

"Mom, they're Ed and Pete," Stephen said in a patronizing tone. "You just met them, and they're my friends."

"They look a lot older than you," Annie said with a concerned frown.

Stephen just shrugged. "See ya, Mom."

"No, Stephen," she replied with a determined set to her jaw. "I forbid you to go!"

"See if you can stop me, then," Stephen said as he pushed passed her.

Annie grabbed onto his blue denim jacket, but Stephen easily pulled away. He was nearly six feet tall and built like his father—tall and broad shouldered. Annie, on the other hand, was an average height but possessed a fuller figure than what most department stores considered average. And though she was strong from working all her life, Annie wasn't stronger than Stephen. There was no way she could physically stop her son.

"Stephen, don't you dare leave this house! I'll call the police again!"

No reply. Annie knew Stephen wouldn't listen, let alone obey. She stepped out of the house and watched her son's retreating back as he walked down the driveway. Then he climbed into the waiting car with his friends. Annie wondered if he'd make it home alive.

She felt so helpless and inept. Stephen was her eldest son, her young man whom she loved with a mother's fierce and protective heart. But he was on the road to self-destruction, and Annie didn't know what to do about it. She had tried teachers, school administrators, counselors, judges, parole officers. However, "The System" had failed Stephen Fetherston. Annie, herself, had failed Stephen. So what or who was left?

Nothing and no one, she decided as she walked back into the house, closing the door behind her.

two

"Can't you control your kid?" Mr. Talbot, one of the neighbors, shouted as he stood at Annie's front door. "I told him twice already not to ride his bike over my lawn, but he still does it!"

"I'm sorry," Annie replied earnestly. "I'll talk to Josh about it."

Mr. Talbot ignored her apology. "I just put new sod in to cover all the tire tracks your kid put on my lawn last summer, and now he's riding over it again!"

"Sorry," Annie told him again. In all her years in customer service, first as a waitress at a bar and grill, then as a receptionist at the paper mill, and now as a cashier at Paradigm Foods, Annie had learned the customer is always right—even though this was Josh's newspaper customer and not hers. "I'll remind Josh to ride on the sidewalk from now on," she told Mr. Talbot, who wore a white T-shirt and denim overalls. "And I know it's not an excuse for what Josh did, but your corner lot is quite a temptation to bicycle riders."

The man glared at Annie. "The fact is, it's my lawn, and I don't want kids riding all over it. So tell your boy that!"

"I will," Annie promised, trying to be diplomatic instead of frustrated.

"And tell him not to throw my newspaper on the front stoop. I want it between the two front doors. When it rains, my paper is all wet and that makes me mad! If that kid would just put it between the doors, I wouldn't have to worry about a wet paper when it rains."

"Sure, I'll tell him."

"And tell him that I'm taking the cost of the ruined sod out of his tip money from now until Christmas."

Annie nodded wearily as Mr. Talbot walked away in a huff. Closing the front door, she turned and leaned against it. She felt as though she had the weight of the whole world on her shoulders at this moment. She had worked all day only to come home to Stephen and his blaring rock and roll and strange-looking friends. . .and now this!

Gazing through the small living room area at Josh, who stood in the kitchen drinking a glass of water, Annie shook her head at him. "Did you hear that?" she asked.

"I heard," Josh replied.

"He said he's keeping your tip money."

Josh shrugged. "That old geezer never tips me anyway, so I don't know what he's talking about."

"Well, just stay off his lawn, will you? I have enough problems with Stephen upsetting the neighbors; I don't need you doing it, too. And you were wrong to ride over Mr. Talbot's lawn—especially since he warned you twice."

Again, Josh shrugged and took a long drink from his glass.

"And you're grounded," Annie said, feeling as though she had to impose some kind of punishment on her youngest boy since he seemed so indifferent about his wrongdoing.

"But, Mom," he cried, and Annie was glad she'd gotten his attention, "I'm supposed to sleep over at Chad's tonight. It's all planned."

"Well, your plans just got cancelled," she replied decisively as she entered the kitchen. "And just for making that neighbor angry enough to come over here and take it out on me, I'm making you go to church tomorrow!"

"What?" Josh's junior high voice broke at the news. "I'm not going to no church!"

"Oh, yes you are!" Annie replied. "And you're going with me. Maybe it'll do you some good—maybe it'll do us both some good!"

"But, Mom—"

Annie whirled on him. "I don't know where I went wrong in raising your brother," she said through a clenched jaw, "but I'm going to make sure that I don't go wrong in raising you! Got it?"

"Got it," Josh replied, though he was obviously not pleased. As if to prove his point, he ran to the stairs, taking them two at a time, and reached his bedroom, slamming the door.

In the kitchen below, Annie breathed a long, heartfelt sigh.

Josh was basically a good kid, and she was desperate to keep him that way. But how? *If I could just figure out what I did so wrong with Stephen,* she mused, *then maybe Josh will be a decent human being when he's sixteen.*

And on that idea she contemplated for the rest of the night, feeling guilty about her failures as a mother and terribly worried over Stephen and his whereabouts.

&

Getting ready for Friend Day the next morning, Annie donned one of the best dresses she owned. It wasn't fancy, but it was a pretty print, tan and russet paisleys against a black background. Annie didn't have a lot of money, but she had nice clothes. She had learned early how to shop prudently, mostly at rummage sales and resale shops. Her mother had always said that Annie had an eye for fashion as well as a good bargain, and over the years, out of necessity, Annie proved her mother correct.

Once she was dressed, Annie marveled that she didn't have to say more than two words to Josh about getting ready for church. For some reason, he had resigned himself to going. Apparently it was only Annie who was balking at this church idea even if she was balking silently.

Stephen had come home at five o'clock in the morning. Annie had met him at the door. They argued, then Stephen left again, and now Annie didn't feel like going to church or anywhere else for that matter. Except what was the alternative? Stay home and worry and feel guilty? She'd done that all night long and it had gotten her nowhere. *Besides, I promised the Winstons,* Annie reminded herself.

Nevertheless, she told herself that she was nuts to do this as she walked to church with Josh by her side. Annie didn't own a car; she didn't have extra money for gas, insurance, and daily upkeep. But, fortunately, she lived in a part of town that was fairly centralized. Annie could reach everything in about a fifteen-minute walk. And the Winstons' church was no exception. It was only about six blocks away.

"We never go to church, Mom," Josh was saying. "Why are we all of a sudden going now?"

"Oh, I promised Maggy Winston."

"Why did you do that?"

"Because it's Friend Day," Annie said pointedly, "and I guess I'm her friend. Besides, a promise is a promise. Right?"

"Right," Josh replied grudgingly. Then he looked over at her. "Is this church like that last church we were in?"

Annie shook her head. "No. The last church we were in was when Grandpa died," she said, speaking of her father, who had passed away some eight years ago. "And I think you were too young to remember that. Daddy's funeral wasn't held in a church. That you would remember. Do you?"

"Sort of."

"The funeral home took care of the memorial service," Annie reminded him. "It was held in something called the 'Chapel Room'."

"Oh, yeah! I remember. . .kind of. . ."

Annie smiled lovingly at her son. "Well, you were only seven when your daddy died."

Josh nodded. "I don't even remember what he looked like."

Annie felt a pinch of guilt. Maybe she had been wrong, she wasn't sure, but the year after Eric died, Annie gave all his clothes and personal effects to charity. Then she had packed away all the family photo albums. She'd packed away all the framed portraits, too—the ones that included Eric, anyway. It was as though she didn't want him hanging on the walls, watching her fail miserably without him.

"I've got two boxes packed full of pictures of you and your dad," Annie told Josh. "I packed one for you and one for Stephen. If you want," she stated haltingly, "I'll give them to you when we get home today. I mean, they are yours. You should have them."

Josh only nodded.

At last they reached the church, located on King Street and, just as John had promised yesterday, Maggy was waiting for them in the vestibule.

"Annie, I'm so glad you came. And this must be Josh."

Annie nodded and introduced her son, even though they had seen each other once or twice before when Josh came into Paradigm Foods.

"You walked, didn't you?" Maggy observed with a little

frown of concern marring her golden brows. "I should have had John pick you up."

"It was only a few blocks," Annie insisted with a polite smile.

"It was almost eight blocks," Josh blurted. "Eight long blocks, too."

Again Annie smiled, but she silenced Josh with a gentle nudge of her elbow to his ribs.

He frowned at her.

Maggy Winston chuckled softly. Then she whispered to Annie, "You look tired."

"I am," Annie replied honestly. "Stephen. Need I say more?"

Maggy shook her head, looking sad. "John and I are praying for him, Annie. Just like we're praying for you."

"Oh. . ."

Annie wasn't sure how to take that. Was it an insult? Or a confirmation that she was a bad mother?

"Well, if you're ready, we can go sit down," Maggy said. "John and the girls are holding a place for us. Our baby is in the nursery."

Annie nodded and followed her. Josh trailed reluctantly. They walked up the center aisle of the small, but modern-looking auditorium, and two pews from the front, Maggy stopped.

"We're sitting way up here?" Annie asked, feeling slightly intimidated.

Maggy nodded. "Do you mind? We always sit up front."

Annie shrugged. She was a guest. How could she say she would prefer a pew in the back row without being rude? Simply, she couldn't.

Josh slid into the pew first, taking a seat beside John. Then Annie sat down, and Maggy took the place next to her. John made the appropriate introductions; his two daughters sat on the other side of him. Annie nodded and smiled at the girls. Josh folded his arms, looking disinterested.

Then Maggy began talking about their church and how the auditorium had been renovated last year.

"We added the choir loft. . .see it? Behind the pulpit?"

Annie nodded and watched as people began filling the chairs.

"You said you don't have much of a church background, isn't that right?"

Again, Annie nodded. "My parents weren't very religious, although we went to church on Christmas and at Easter." She looked away from the choir members now and turned to Maggy. "You know, I always thought of God as being like the Wizard of Oz," she finally confessed, wearing an amused smile. "Remember the big white face that made the Scarecrow shake and scared Dorothy till her knees knocked and frightened the Lion so he jumped out the window?"

Maggy chuckled softly. "Oh, Annie, that's so funny. But it's so far from the truth. The Bible says that God created mankind in His image. And Jesus was a Man who walked this earth just as we do. He had feelings—He laughed and cried, and Jesus is the Son of God! Definitely more than just a big white face!"

"Hmmm. . ."

Annie furrowed her brows pensively, trying to take in all of what Maggy said. God a Man? Walking around on earth? It all seemed very confusing, since she had had such a different idea of who God was. Then, again, Annie often felt confused after talking to Maggy about God.

Maggy once told her that there were three parts to God: God the Father, God the Son, and God the Holy Spirit. That had thrown Annie for a loop until she finally figured that those three parts to God were probably like her favorite trilogy— different stories, but the same characters. And all three books belonged together, but each one had to be read separately.

Piano music suddenly began to play, pulling Annie out of her thoughts. Looking in the direction of the sleek, black grand piano, which was off to one side, Annie saw the man playing it. He had sandy blond hair and wore a double-breasted, black-and-white tweed suit. Annie smiled, thinking the man matched his piano quite nicely. And, though she couldn't see his face very well, she began to sense the man and his piano were much more than a nice match. He seemed to be caught up in the melody he was playing—as though he were feeling every note he played.

"That's Dan Brenshaw," Maggy whispered, leaning toward Annie. "He's currently our music director, and he helps with the youth group. But he's only on loan to us till January."

"Oh," Annie replied, nodding politely.

"We're blessed to have him, too," Maggy added. "Dan is very educated. He has a degree in music and another in theology. He's also part of the Mike Pettit Evangelistic Team."

Annie frowned. "What's an evangelistic team?"

Maggy smiled patiently. "It's a group of people who travel around the world and preach the gospel."

"I see." At least Annie thought she did; she'd never heard of an evangelistic team before.

"Anyway," Maggy continued, "Dan has been here since June, helping our church and Christian day school staff revive their music departments."

"Oh, well, that's nice," Annie said for lack of a better reply. However, she had to admit that what she was hearing now, from that piano man, was one hundred times better than anything coming out of Stephen's stereo!

Annie listened closer. It was a beautiful melody, and slowly the music began to affect her in a strange and remarkable way. It both soothed her and moved her.

"What's the name of this. . .this melody?" Annie asked.

" 'Be Thou My Vision'," Maggy replied with a sweet smile. "Do you like it?"

Annie nodded. "Can a person get a record or a tape of piano music like this?"

"Sure. The music store in the mall has plenty of them. But Dan's got some of his own cassette tapes. We can ask him for one after the service."

"Oh, that's all right," Annie replied quickly. "I don't want to. . .to bother him." The truth of the matter was, Annie didn't have the extra funds to buy a music tape.

"It's no bother, Annie. Dan loves to share his music."

Annie smiled. "Thanks, but maybe another time, Maggy."

She nodded agreeably.

Just then, the piano man began to play another tune. It was a slower, more heartfelt melody. Suddenly a lovely young woman was standing behind the podium, her black hair shining under the auditorium lights. She announced that the song she was about to sing was a classic American folk hymn that first appeared in William Walker's *Southern Harmony* back in 1835. Then the piano man began to play and she began to sing:

> What wondrous love is this, O my soul, O my soul!
> What wondrous love is this, O my soul!
> What wondrous love is this that caused the Lord of
> bliss to bear the dreadful curse for my soul, for
> my soul, to bear the dreadful curse for my soul. . .

As Annie listened, something clicked for her: God—Jesus, a man—bore a dreadful curse for. . .for whose soul? Christians? And that's why they worship Him and love Him so much?

The song ended then, and the dark-haired lady sat down.

"That was Nancy Taylor," Maggy said. "Doesn't she have a beautiful singing voice?"

Annie nodded. She had never heard one better.

"Dan has all the soloists announce their music before they sing." Maggy smiled. "He's trying to educate us."

Annie smiled back as the pastor stood up at the pulpit. Everyone stood for what was called the opening prayer. Then there was more music. An entire half hour filled with music. Annie thought it was a wonderful way to spend the time in church. Now this kind of church she could attend every day!

But her gladness was short-lived when the pastor took the pulpit again. Maggy said his name was Ashford. Pastor Ashford. And all Annie seemed to hear of his sermon was sin, sin, sin and hell, hell, hell.

I don't need to sit here and listen to somebody I never met before tell me what a bad person I am, she thought. *I'm a rotten mother, and I was probably a rotten wife, too.*

Pastor Ashford finally finished his message, and Annie held back a sigh of relief. Then he asked the congregation to bow their heads, saying, "If you're here today and want to know for sure that you're on your way to heaven, raise your hand and someone will be glad to show you, from the Bible, how you can be saved. Right here. Right now."

From the corner of her eye, Annie saw Josh lift his hand. Startled, she nudged him.

"What are you doing?" she whispered.

"I don't want to got to hell, Mom," he answered with a glint of fear in his eyes.

Before Annie could reply, John was encouraging him to step out of the pew with him. Then the piano man began to play a slow, sad-sounding melody.

"Where is John taking him?" Annie asked Maggy with some concern.

"Just to a quiet, private corner where they can talk. John is going to show Josh from the Bible how he can be saved."

"And then what?"

"And then he's saved."

"For how long?"

"Forever, Annie. That's why it's called eternal life. Isn't that exciting?"

Annie didn't know if it was exciting or not. Did Josh join this church when he got saved? Would she have to pay a certain amount of money every month in order to keep him "saved forever"?

Within minutes, the service ended and the music stopped. Pastor Ashford closed with a prayer and then more music began to play. This time it was lighthearted and happy sounding. People left their pews and filled the aisles, talking, laughing, and smiling as they greeted each other. Annie was introduced to several of Maggy's friends, and then Josh and John Winston appeared. They were both smiling broadly.

"Okay, so tell your mom what happened," John prompted.

Josh shrugged, looking embarrassed. "I got saved," he said.

"Well, good," Annie replied, though she was still puzzled about so many things concerning God and salvation. "So now your grades will go up, and you'll be a model twelve-year-old. Right?"

"No. . .I don't know," Josh said in all his chagrin as the Winstons chuckled.

"Come on," said John, "let's celebrate by going out to lunch. My treat."

"Can we, Mom?" Josh asked with a hopefulness in his brown eyes that Annie hadn't seen for a long, long time.

She nodded. "We can go. And thanks, John."

"My pleasure. I'm glad you both came today." With his arm around Maggy, John gave her an affectionate squeeze. Then over his shoulder he said to Annie, "I hope you'll come again."

Annie just shrugged in reply. She wasn't sure if she'd come back or not. Maybe she would. . .just to hear that piano man play. That half hour of music and singing had done her more good than a hot bubble bath after a busy day!

As they headed for the auditorium's doorway, Annie sensed there was something very different about her son now. . .now that he was saved. It was the oddest sense, too—as if Josh didn't belong to her anymore and the course of his life was no longer her choosing. And that idea frightened Annie a little bit because she had already lost one son—he was spinning out of control like an ungrounded kite in the wind. Was she really going to lose Josh, too?

three

The following morning, Annie awoke to the autumn sunshine pouring through her eastern bedroom window. Her tumultuous feelings from yesterday morning were gone, since Josh seemed to be back to normal. Actually, yesterday afternoon had been a relatively pleasant one. John had taken them out to lunch with Maggy and their kids, then he'd deposited her and Josh at home, where they spent a lazy, fall afternoon watching a football game. Stephen had even come home later on and, though he seemed withdrawn throughout supper, he didn't make any trouble. Maybe things were going to be all right after all.

Annie yawned and stretched. Today was Monday, the second day of her weekend since she worked Tuesdays through Saturdays, and today was hers! She'd clean a little and putter around a lot. She'd get the laundry and the dishes done and then get her hair done—Annie's one and only luxury. A friend, Charlene Hughes, cut Annie's hair and gave her a permanent free of charge. In return, Annie cleaned Char's house, since Char had back problems and cleaning her house only aggravated her condition. So it was a fair trade, once every six weeks or so, and Annie enjoyed Char's company.

Still in bed, Annie suddenly tuned into the sound of her boys arguing over who got to use the bathroom first. It appeared that Josh was trying to hold his ground while Stephen was pulling rank.

"Get outta my way, punk!" Stephen demanded.

"You get outta my way, jerk!" Josh replied.

Stephen began spewing out an array of nasty adjectives, but then suddenly things got quiet. Annie threw back the bedcovers, anticipating a full-fledged war. She grabbed her robe and tied it at the waist as she headed toward the bathroom where the two boys stood, glaring angrily at each other.

"Get out of the bathroom," Stephen told Josh.

"Forget it. I was here first."

"You're a nerd. Know that?"

"Yeah?" Josh said, lifting his chin defiantly. "Well, at least I'm not going to hell like you!"

Annie stopped short, her eyes wide. Then she noticed that even Stephen looked surprised at the remark.

"That's enough, boys," Annie told them both, yet wondering over her youngest's remark. There was that little bit of change in him again, a kind of certainty that he had about his destiny. "Josh gets the bathroom, Stephen," she said diplomatically. "I was listening, so I know he got in there first."

"Ha, ha," Josh told his brother as he shut the door.

Annie sighed, shaking her head. Whatever little bit of change she'd seen in Josh only moments before seemed to have vanished before her very eyes.

Stephen, however, angrily smacked the door with his palm. Then he went into his bedroom, slamming the door.

Annie sighed again, wishing she were back in her warm bed with a pillow over her head. Moments later and halfway down the stairs, Annie heard the boom-de-boom-boom coming from Stephen's stereo. *Oh no,* she thought. *He's playing that dreadful stuff he calls music again!*

"Turn it down, Stephen," Annie called, coming back up the steps. "Turn it down!"

As Stephen opened the door, the music grew louder. "What?"

"Turn it down! That noise makes me nervous, Stephen. I can't imagine what it's doing to you!"

He grinned mischievously and then pretended to play the guitar along with the one screaming in the background.

"Stephen, please!" Annie said, covering her ears. That hard, acid rock and roll bothered her as much as fingernails down a chalkboard. Even more!

Finally he went back into his room and turned down his stereo. In the kitchen, Annie was shaking as she fixed a pot of coffee. Why did she even bother? It wasn't as if she needed the caffeine; her nerves were already strung tight as a whipcord.

It's that music, she decided. It could make a person crazy!

Walking to the portable radio/cassette player that stood on the counter beside the toaster, Annie searched the FM band for something to offset the *boom boom boom* coming through the ceiling. Finally she settled on the morning news.

❧

"Your hair is really getting long, Annie," Char said, rolling it for the permanent wave. Annie had been wearing her blondish-brown hair the same way for years: chin-length all the way around, except the bangs. The perm just made it fuller and wavier.

"If you think my hair is getting long," Annie replied, "you should see Stephen's!" She shook her head at the mention of her wayward boy. "He wears it in a ponytail."

Charlene didn't seem shocked in the least. "Oh, that's the style these days," she said. "A ponytail is fashionable on young men."

Annie shrugged, supposing it might be a trendy thing; however, she kept imagining what Eric would say if he were alive and could see his son today. He'd most likely consider Stephen a "flunky," which was, unfortunately, a close reality—and it had nothing to do with his ponytail, either. Just this morning the school called to report that Stephen hadn't shown up for class—again. But Annie had seen him board the school bus. So where did he go after he'd gotten off?

Probably with Pink Top Pete in that car, Annie surmised. And now Stephen would be reported as truant, and then his probation officer may or may not follow through on his threat to incarcerate Stephen. A "lock-in" school, he had called it, one in which Stephen would be forced to attend classes. He would be locked in all week long with visits only allowed on the weekends, although if his behavior warranted it, he might be granted leaves to come home. Annie had been opposed to the lock-in idea, but now she wondered if it wasn't the best thing. She was that desperate.

Once her hair was rolled and the strong-smelling solution applied, Annie wrapped her head in a plastic cap, provided by the perm kit, and began cleaning. Char followed her around, helping with the dusting and putting things away.

"Annie, I don't know what I'd do without you," Char said. "You're a godsend. I mean, if I had to hire a cleaning lady to do all my heavy once-a-month jobs, I'd go broke!"

"Well, Char, I know what I'd do without you," Annie teased.

"I'd be walking all over town with straight out-of-fashion hair, that's what I'd be doing!"

Char laughed, Annie joined her, and so it went for the next several hours. But by four o'clock, Annie was back home, making supper. Josh finished his paper route and announced, as he burst through the back door, that he hadn't even used the shortcut across Mr. Talbot's new sod.

"That's good," Annie said, noting that little bit of difference in her son again—that "something" from yesterday.

"But I only did it cuz I didn't want him yelling at you again, Mom," Josh added.

Annie turned from the casserole she'd been preparing. "You did it for me, Josh?"

He shrugged. "Sure. You're my mom, aren't you? Somebody's gotta look after you."

Annie frowned, her defenses rising, and put her hands on her hips. "I think I can look after myself just fine, thank you very much."

Josh shrugged again, and Annie sensed he was suffering from that "I want to be a man" syndrome that was chronic at his age. Stephen used to say things like that, too—like he wanted to protect his mother.

But things change, Annie decided, sliding the casserole into the oven. Now all Stephen did was hurt her with his rebelliousness. Then all at once it occurred to her that perhaps she had somehow discouraged Stephen from doing the good things, like protecting her, by exerting her independence.

"Josh," she suddenly called, stopping him as he reached the stairs, "I've changed my mind—you can look after me all you want. I. . .I think I need that."

He didn't reply, but Annie saw a little grin form on his face just before he climbed the steps.

❧

Later that evening, after supper dishes were washed and put away, Annie sent Josh upstairs to do his homework. Stephen still hadn't come home, and Annie decided that he had until midnight before she'd call the police and report him missing.

Turning on the television, Annie decided to make a night of watching a movie. But then, just as she was settled into the sofa, the doorbell rang.

Annie's first inclination was not to answer it; it could be another raving neighbor. On the other hand, it might be the police with news of Stephen's whereabouts. She peeked out the window, but didn't see any squad cars. Back to the raving neighbor guess.

The doorbell rang again, and Josh bounded down the steps. He looked at his mother with questioning eyes. "I thought maybe you were in the basement doing laundry or something," he said, obviously because she hadn't answered the door.

Annie shook her head. "I've been here. . .but since you're my protector, how about seeing who's ringing our doorbell?"

Josh grinned sheepishly. "Okay."

He walked into the small front hallway, opened the door, and Annie heard a male voice greet him. Then Josh replied, "Oh, hi, Mr. Winston."

Annie got up off the couch, straightened her multicolored, pullover sweater, which she wore over faded blue jeans, and walked to where Josh stood with the door wide open.

"Ask him in, Josh," Annie told him.

He did, but as John stepped into the house, another man followed. He looked vaguely familiar to Annie, and then she recognized him as Deerwood Bible Church's piano man. Except, unlike yesterday morning, Annie could see his face clearly now that he stood in her living room.

She decided it was a nice face, in spite of its somewhat ruddy complexion. The wide, almond-shaped, teal blue eyes added a softness to what might otherwise be the countenance of a hard-looking man. Then, in two sweeping glances, Annie noticed the man's burgundy leather jacket, which he wore open over a navy blue and white sweater, dark blue jeans, and. . .and sneakers! High-tops, to be exact! And they looked as if they had seen better days, too!

Annie fought to hide her smile as she found the combination of a fine leather jacket and worn-out sneakers both amusing and disarming. And in just those few seconds, Annie decided he was a nice, no nonsense, no pretense, sort of guy.

"Hi, Annie," John said with a friendly smile as he tousled Josh's light brown hair. "Dan and I are out visiting folks with teenagers tonight, so we thought we'd pop in on you and Josh."

"Oh, well. . .thanks," she replied simply.

"Dan, this is Annie Fetherston and her son Josh and, you two, this is Dan Brenshaw."

"Hi," Josh said as Dan offered his hand in a welcoming shake.

"Nice to meet you, Josh."

Annie thought her son looked pleased that an adult should be so respectful to a mere child. Many adults weren't, Annie knew, and somehow kids could sense that.

Then he turned the same greeting on Annie. "Nice to meet you, too, Mrs. Fetherston."

Annie shook his hand but just smiled a reply. She felt suddenly embarrassed, mostly because she hadn't been expecting company, and her house wasn't exactly prepared for this little visit. Sunday's newspaper was still spread out over the coffee table, and Josh's backpack was on the floor by the television set. But, on the other hand, Annie knew John Winston wouldn't judge her for her home's lived-in condition, and the piano man didn't seem the judgmental type, either.

"You guys want to sit down?" Annie asked, feeling more at ease now.

John, however, shook his head. "No, we can only stay a minute or two." Then he pulled a postcard-like thing from his dark green down jacket pocket. "Our youth group is sponsoring a pizza party on Wednesday night, and we were wondering if Josh can come." He handed the postcard to Josh.

"But I'm not a teenager yet," he said, frowning at the invitation.

John replied, "You're eligible to join once you're in junior high. Are you in junior high?"

Josh thought it over. "I'm in seventh grade, so I guess that's junior high."

"It is indeed," John said with a broad grin. "So, what do you say, Annie?"

"I don't know," she replied reluctantly. "A party on a school night?"

"He'll be home by nine o'clock," John promised. "Besides,"

he added with a mischievous grin, "all of us youth group workers are having a contest. Whoever gets the most people to come out on Wednesday night goes out to dinner Saturday for free. . .at the expense of the other workers!" John grinned.

Annie couldn't help but smile. "It's a contest, huh?"

"Yep, and it's a tie so far between John and me," Dan said with a sportive smile. "A tie by one card."

"Aw, too bad I'm sad," John told him with a glint of humor in his eyes. Then to Annie, he said, "Dan usually wins these things. But not this time."

"Oh," she replied lamely. She had never heard of a contest like this.

"Hey," Dan said, snapping his fingers at his latest idea, "are adults allowed to come to this thing?"

John nodded. "Sure. Parents are supposed to come."

In the next instant, Dan was handing a card to Annie. "And make sure you print your name at the top and then my name on the bottom there, where it says invited by."

"Uh-oh," Annie said, feigning a worried expression. "John is my boss. I can't very well be a traitor."

Dan shook his sandy-blond head. "All's fair in youth group competitions, Mrs. Fetherston," he informed her. "Isn't that right, John?"

John gave him a quelling look. "They were both supposed to go on my invitation card, Dan."

He shrugged. "Sorry, pal, I got to her first."

Annie rolled her eyes, for some odd reason feeling flattered. "Well, I'll let you guys slug it out," she said in jest, "outside of my house, that is. But, okay, Josh and I will come to the pizza party."

Both men smiled, looking pleased with the outcome.

Then, after she showed John and Dan to the door, Annie turned to Josh and asked, "What did I just agree to here?"

He grinned. "I don't know, Mom, but this card says it's all-you-can-eat pizza on Wednesday night, and that's all that matters to me!"

four

The Fetherstons were the last visit of the night and, on the way to dropping Dan off at his apartment, John suggested they stop for a cup of coffee at the corner doughnut shop. Dan agreed, so John made a left at the stoplight and pulled his mini-van into the parking lot.

Climbing out of the mini-van, they entered the shop, which was empty, save for one man sitting in a corner booth reading a newspaper. Dan and John selected counter seats, removed their jackets, and sat down. The waitress came over promptly, and the two men ordered hot coffee, John requesting his decaffeinated.

"So, what's her story?" Dan asked, stirring a packet of sugar into his cup. "I know you said the boy got saved yesterday."

"You mean Annie?"

Dan nodded. "She's not a believer. Isn't that what you said?"

This time John nodded. "But Maggy and I are praying to that end." He smiled. "Annie has been working for us for almost a year. She's a good employee, always on time, never sick."

"Divorced?"

John shook his head. "Widowed. Annie doesn't really talk to me about personal things, but she talks to Maggy. From what I've gathered, Annie's husband died when her boys were pretty young. She's had to work ever since, and because she never finished high school, the jobs she's had weren't the greatest. But somehow she has kept up the mortgage payments, put food on the table, and her boys have the clothes they need. Annie's eldest boy is very rebellious. Maggy said she thinks it's because Annie was working all the time and wasn't around to discipline him."

"Well, it sounds like a hard life, John," Dan replied. "Besides, there are some kids who just make bad decisions regardless of their parents' efforts at discipline. Even happens to Christian kids."

John gave it a moment's thought and then shook his head in agreement.

"So where's her family?"

John shrugged. "To my knowledge, Annie's never mentioned any family."

"Hmm. . ." Dan grew pensive, trying to piece together a mental picture of what Annie Fetherston's life might be like. "How come she hasn't remarried? I mean, if her husband's been dead such a long while?"

Again, John shrugged. "I know it hasn't been for lack of interest. I've overheard male customers ask her out right there in her checkout lane. I've also heard Annie turn them down." John grinned. "She's very sweet about it, though."

"She's got a sweet-sounding voice," Dan remarked, taking a sip of his coffee. He grimaced—the stuff tasted like sludge.

"Bet you're wondering if Annie sings, huh?" John chuckled.

"Yeah, well, does she?"

"Don't know."

Dan shook his head, feigning a disappointed frown.

"Maggy and I think Annie's got a tender heart, though. She's open to the gospel, at least she has been for the past few months. But for some reason neither Maggy nor I have been able to get through to her. Annie never seems to quite understand, but it's not that she's unintelligent. On the contrary, Annie is smart. Maggy says she reads a lot, so that probably accounts for it.

"In my opinion," John continued, "Annie has managerial skills. She's organized and has plenty of common sense. She's good with people. However, her lack of a high school diploma keeps her from moving ahead in the business world."

"Probably for the best," Dan said facetiously as he poured another packet of sugar into his coffee. "The business world has ruined plenty of good women."

John chuckled. Dan could come up with the most outrageous statements every once in a while! "Listen, brother," he told him, "it's a good thing you're in the ministry and not in business."

"Amen!" Dan replied, wearing a sheepish grin. "But, hey, I'm only kidding. I respect a woman's role in the business community as well as in the ministry."

John nodded, knowing that was the truth. Dan Brenshaw was an honest man, even if he was bold as brass and had a smart mouth!

Both men grew quiet then, looking into their coffee cups.

"You as tired as I am, Dan?"

"Exhausted."

John nodded, thinking of how good it would be to go home where Maggy was waiting for him. "So how come you never got married, Dan?" he couldn't help asking now.

Dan shrugged. "Never met the right one, I guess. But before I came to know the Savior, some seventeen years ago, I had all the women I wanted. What did I need to get married for? That's what I thought. Then, after I was born again and grew some in the Lord, I felt Him calling me into the music ministry, so I decided to go to college. I was twenty-two years old then. A late bloomer, but a serious student. I was too busy to get married."

"You earned a couple of degrees, didn't you?" John asked. "I remember hearing you had a degree in music as well as a degree in Bible."

Dan nodded. "I felt I needed to study the Bible in its entirety to be effective in the ministry. I worked odd jobs, and the Lord saw me through. I was thirty-four years old by the time I had finished all my schooling. Then I hooked up with Mike Pettit, and I've been traveling the last four years. And I guess now, just as it was when I was in school, I'm far too busy to have a wife and family."

"But Mike is married, isn't he?"

Dan nodded. "And Ruth is a real jewel in her husband's crown. But all that didn't happen on the road. Happened before Mike even got to grad school." He chuckled. "Ruth snatched him up right quick!"

John was chuckling, too, and thought the same thing he always thought when he conversed with Dan: He's a fun guy and I love to hear him talk!

Dan had the most interesting accent John had ever heard. It sounded like a cross between a Texas twang and an East Coast drawl. . .because it was!

Dan had given his testimony last June, after deciding to stay in Rhinelander for a while. He was born and raised in West Virginia, but moved to Texas during his high school days after his father had gotten a job transfer. Dan had stayed in Texas for college, the first time around. Then, for his degree in Bible, he had gone back East. John guessed that Dan was a true southerner at heart, but everyone at Deerwood Bible Church was glad to have him here, even if it was only temporarily.

When the Mike Pettit Evangelistic Team first came to their church last June, its believers were in desperate need of revival. They got it, too, with Mike's strong preaching straight from the Word of God. And then they got an additional blessing: Dan Brenshaw decided to stay on and help develop a godly music department. His participation in the youth group was simply another aspect of his ministry here, and he was well liked among the teenagers.

It's going to be one sorry day, John decided, when Dan Brenshaw leaves Rhinelander.

&

When John finally got home, it was nearly ten o'clock. He and Maggy closed the store every night at five for the specific reason of church participation. Monday night visitation was part of that, and God always blessed them for the sacrifice, even though John's competitors might argue their reasons for staying open—some even for twenty-four hours a day, seven days a week. However, John ran his business according to what he felt were biblical principles, not worldly values, and he had never been sorry—only spiritually enhanced.

As he walked through the kitchen of their single-story ranch-style home, all was quiet. John paused to check on his children, sending up a silent prayer for each of them. The three children, Eliza, age thirteen; Katie, eleven; and baby Noah, not quite a year, were all sleeping peacefully.

Then he entered the master bedroom where Maggy was already in bed, reading a book.

"How did it go?" she asked immediately as John entered the room.

"All the visits went fine," John replied, loosening his tie and unbuttoning his white shirt.

"I meant with Annie," Maggy said, narrowing her gaze. "And you know what I meant."

John grinned. He knew. "Well, the good news is Annie agreed to come Wednesday night, and Josh is coming, too."

"That's great!"

"Dan invited her and she said yes. I don't know how he did it."

"Maybe he didn't," Maggy said, lifting a pretty winged brow. "Maybe God did it."

"No doubt," John agreed. "But He used Dan to do it!"

With that, John leaned over and kissed his wife.

☙

Stephen came home just after eleven o'clock that night. His eyes were bloodshot, and he smelled of cigarette smoke and beer. When Annie questioned him, he got defensive and yelled at her. Finally he threw a water goblet across the kitchen. It hit the cupboard near the telephone and shattered. Then Stephen refused to clean up the mess.

With tears of frustration building behind her eyes, Annie picked up the bigger pieces of glass and then vacuumed the floor. Afterward, she gathered her wits and climbed the steps to Stephen's room where his music blared from within. She knocked. Knocked again. Then finally she opened the door and walked in. Stephen never heard her enter, nor did he hear her as she walked to the stereo. . .until she turned it off.

"Hey!"

"Hey, nothing. You and I have to talk."

"Forget it." But when Stephen went to turn his music back on, Annie pulled the plug out of the wall.

"If you don't talk to me right now," she warned, "I'll pull this cord out of that machine and it'll never work again."

Stephen paused in his tracks. Finally Annie had his attention.

"What's happened to you, Stephen?" she began. "You used to be such a nice boy. We used to get along so well. Remember when we used to go sit by the river and I taught you how to fish?"

Stephen folded his arms, looking disinterested.

"If I did something to make you hate me—"

"Lay off the guilt trip, Mom!"

"But I must have done something."

Stephen rolled his eyes.

Realizing she was getting nowhere, Annie decided to try a different approach. "Doesn't it concern you that because you didn't show up at school today you could go to jail? That lock-in school?"

"I ain't scared of jail," the young man sneered. "The cops'll have to find me first, anyway, and they won't. My friends'll see to that."

"So you're just going to hide out all your life?" Annie shook her head in disappointment. "What about college? A career? What about a future? Have you given that any thought?"

"I gotta live for today, Mom," Stephen replied. "A man's only young once. I've watched you work for years. . .for nothing. You think I wanna do that?"

Annie couldn't believe what she was hearing. She'd done it all for him, and Stephen was throwing it back in her face.

"No way!" he continued. "I wanna live. Enjoy life. Enjoy my friends. Girls."

"Girls?" Annie frowned; she hoped fervently that she wasn't going to be a grandmother any time soon.

Stephen looked at her as if she was the dumbest person alive. "Yes, girls, Mom. Boys and girls—they go together. Relationships. That's what life is all about."

Annie was shaking her head sadly. "Oh, Stephen. . ."

"Hey, you think I want to be lonely all my life like you? What do you have in your life? Nothing. And no one. But I've got friends and more friends. I'm alive," he said emphatically. "But you're just existing!"

Trying to hold back the incredible hurt and heartache Stephen had inflicted upon her was useless. Annie broke down. She sagged to the edge of Stephen's extra twin bed and cried into the palms of her hands. Stephen, in his indifference, plugged the stereo back into the wall socket. And then the sounds that filled the room were so terrible—like wounded, dying animals—that Annie couldn't stand to stay there.

꙰

For the next two days, Annie was solemn and quiet. John noticed. Maggy noticed. But Annie couldn't seem to get herself to open up to them. She was so hurt to have discovered what her own son thought of her that it made her feel ashamed somehow. Was Stephen's opinion the general consensus of the community? Of her employers? Did people really pity her and use her as an example of how not to live their lives?

"I hope you and Josh are still planning to come tonight," Maggy said on Wednesday as Annie was ringing out.

"I don't know."

"What's wrong? You haven't been yourself lately. Is it your son again?"

"Yes. But it's me, too, Maggy."

"What do you mean?"

Annie only shook her head. That's as far as she thought she could go right now.

"I think you'll feel better if you get out and have some fun. You'll meet some new people—"

"Maggy, are you saying that I'm little better than a cadaver?"

She frowned. "What?"

"Well, that's what Stephen thinks. He said all I do is work, work, work, and I don't have any friends. And. . .well, maybe it's true. Except for visiting my girlfriend Charlene once in a while, I don't have much of a social life. And you've noticed it. I mean, ever since I started working here, you and John have been pushing me to do all sorts of church things. Maybe it's obvious to everyone but me that my life is. . .is empty. Dead."

Annie only had to glance at Maggy and her shocked expression to realize she'd said too much. She had hurt Maggy now and, deep inside, Annie knew Maggy was only trying to help.

"Oh, I'm sorry, Maggy. I guess I'm just feeling sorry for myself."

After a long pause, Maggy replied, "If my son ever said anything like that to me, I'd give him a good spanking! No matter how old he was!"

Now it was Annie's turn to be surprised. Then she grinned at the ridiculous, mind's-eye vision of herself trying to spank Stephen. He was at least five inches taller. He was bigger and stronger. And, imagining Stephen hanging over her knees for a spanking, Annie laughed aloud.

"Well, that's better," Maggy said, with a smile of her own. She took Annie's cash drawer from her and then added, "I'll see you tonight. Right?"

Annie hesitated. She knew Josh wanted to go and eat pizza to his heart's content. "Right," she said at last. "I'll be there."

five

Annie had to hurry and get dressed. She had been in her bathrobe, having changed her mind again about going to the pizza party. Annie figured she just wouldn't show up. She would explain later. Maggy would understand.

But then, as if by Divine Inspiration, Maggy called and insisted on picking up Annie and Josh. Annie felt caught; she had said she would go so she had to make good on her word and yet she didn't want to have to meet anyone and try to socialize.

"I should have just said no." Annie grumbled, pulling on a long denim skirt over which she wore a white turtleneck and lavender sweater with pink and white embroidered flowers around the neckline. Blue stockings and blue leather pumps and she was all set.

"Are you ready, Josh?"

"Yep," he answered from behind a bicycle magazine.

Stephen was gone. Annie hadn't really seen him since Monday night, though she knew he had been in and out of the house. The school had called yesterday and today—Stephen hadn't shown up for any of his classes. Annie had all but given up on him, wondering again if jail wasn't the best alternative.

A horn sounded, and Annie and Josh grabbed their fall jackets, heading for the front door. Annie locked it on the way out.

"We're so glad you could come," Maggy said as they climbed into the van.

For lack of another seat, Josh had to sit next to one of the Winstons' girls. He looked at his mother and wrinkled his nose in distaste, causing Annie to smile. He was still so much of a little boy at times. If only he would stay that way.

Annie thought of Stephen, whose interests centered around his horrid music, girls, and "relationships." She cringed inwardly, thinking of the teen pregnancy crisis in the country and hoping vehemently that her son wasn't contributing to it. What a helpless feeling it was for Annie to realize that somehow, somewhere, she had lost parental control of her eldest son.

The van turned into the church parking lot, and when it stopped, the kids jumped out. Maggy picked the baby up out of his car seat, and then she and Annie followed John and the others into the building.

The party was being held in the lower level, in a large room with yellow-painted concrete block walls and cream-colored linoleum tiles on the floor. Long tables with orange and gold paper coverings lined the center of the room, and permeating the air was the unmistakable smell of pizza.

Several minutes passed noisily until the pastor appeared and called for silence. Then he prayed, asking God's blessing on the food, after which everyone was encouraged to help themselves buffet style, and a line formed.

Like a wallflower, Annie stood on one side of the room and watched the goings-on around her. The teens were clean-cut young men and well-groomed young women. Josh looked shaggy by comparison. And then a vague uneasiness settled down around Annie as she thought that perhaps the parents of these teens had done all the things right that she had done wrong.

But what specifically? she wondered. Surely these kids had their rebellious moments. So how did their parents handle them?

Annie continued watching the teenagers and parents alike until finally it became an unbearable sight, though she couldn't look away. Somehow the mothers here represented the woman Annie always thought she was, but so obviously wasn't. The teens here were the kinds of kids Annie had so long ago dreamed her sons would be, but weren't. And suddenly an overwhelming sense of discouragement loomed over her head like a great, dark storm cloud.

"Hi, Mrs. Fetherston. Glad you could make it. Did you fill out that invitation card just like I said?"

Turning, Annie came face-to-grinning-face with Dan Brenshaw.

"Aren't you going to eat any pizza?" he asked, looking concerned. "Best get it while it's hot. And while it's there! These kids have mean appetites!"

Annie nodded for lack of anything to say.

Dan paused, considering her briefly. "Pardon my asking, but are you feeling okay? You look troubled."

Annie shook her head a bit too quickly. "It's just been a long week."

"I hear ya!" he drawled cordially. "Life can sure get hectic when we let it."

Annie forced a smile and nodded once more.

Dan folded his arms and leaned against the wall. Annie looked straight ahead at nothing in particular, but she sensed the man's intrusive gaze and wished he'd go talk to someone else.

"Mrs. Fetherston," he said in a low, earnest tone, "I hope you won't think badly of John Winston for this, and of me for saying it, but he told me you're having some problems with your eldest boy."

Surprised, Annie turned to look at him.

"I think I can help you," he added, "or at least direct you to the One who can."

Annie swallowed a hard lump of sudden emotion. On one hand, she wanted to refuse this man's help, but on the other, she didn't think she could afford to. He stood waiting for an answer, yes or no, take the offer or don't.

"Thanks," Annie said. "I'd like to hear anything you might suggest."

"Then, why don't we step over to that back table," Dan suggested, pointing across the room. The card table was small and square and, conveniently, two empty chairs stood beside it.

Annie followed Dan as half a dozen things ran through her head. *What kind of help? I've probably tried it already. Does this guy know what sort of problems I'm having with Stephen? Probably not. How could he if all he deals with are well-adjusted teens like the ones in this room?*

Dan pulled the first chair out for her, and Annie was slightly surprised by the gesture. *How long had it been since* a man held a chair for her? Too long, her heart replied.

Annie sat down, and Dan walked around the table, taking the other chair. Then he opened his Bible, and Annie realized he must have been holding it the entire time. So this was the help he was talking about.

"Before I show you a couple of verses here, let me just tell you something about me. Okay?"

Annie shrugged, feeling a pinch of disappointment. What could he say that the Winstons hadn't already said?

"Before I asked Jesus into my heart," Dan began, "I was about as rebellious as they come. I did manage to graduate from high school, but just barely. From there I decided to be a rock and roll star." He grinned at the memory, as if acknowledging its foolishness. "I wanted my name in lights, and I wanted my music to hit the charts like dynamite. But you know where my ambition took me? It took me into some of the most wicked, vile places a man could ever go." Dan shook his head ruefully. "By the time I was twenty years old, I was doing drugs every day and boozing every night. By then I couldn't even make my music anymore because of my altered mental state, and it wasn't long before I hit ground zero."

Annie's attention had now been won, and she felt a new sense of hope. "I think my son. . .well, he's not a musician, but I think he's heading in that same direction."

Dan nodded. "I thought maybe that was the case." He opened his Bible then. "Now, Mrs. Fetherston, if you want to help your son, you have to help yourself first. The truth is, your son needs to know God's Son, Jesus Christ—only you've got to know Him first."

Dan pointed to his Bible, and said, "There are three things God wants you to know. First, you need to be saved. The Bible says, 'For all have sinned and come short of the glory of God.' " He looked up. "Do you know you're a sinner?"

Annie nodded. She thought of herself as a bad mother, and she supposed that was enough sin for any person. But even so, she couldn't say that she never told a lie. She couldn't say she never broke any of the Ten Commandments, and Maggy had said that anyone who broke the Ten Commandments was a sinner.

"Yes," Annie said softly, guiltily. "I know."

"Good!" Dan declared.

"Good?" Annie gave him a quizzical look.

He just nodded. "On to the second thing God wants you to know and that is—you can't save yourself." He flipped a few pages back. "The Bible says, 'Jesus saith. . .I am the way, the truth, and the life: no man cometh unto the Father, but by Me.'

"See, it's like you're on the one side of the Grand Canyon, Mrs. Fetherston, and God is on the other side. You can't reach Him. But since Jesus Christ laid down His life for all mankind, He's become our bridge to God."

Annie thought it over and understood the illustration clearly. She couldn't reach God because she was a sinner, but Jesus Christ bridged the gap because He was that second part of God, just as Maggy had talked about.

"Okay," she said.

Dan grinned. "Okay! Now the third thing God wants you to know is that salvation is a gift and anyone can have this gift. You can't earn salvation by being good and helping little old ladies across the street, although it's nice if you do."

Annie smiled.

"But you can be saved today. Right now, in fact. Jesus Christ loves you, and He wants you to come to Him in faith, trusting that He alone can save you." Dan smiled. "You see, all you have to do is ask."

Annie lifted a surprised brow. "That's it?"

Dan nodded. "That's it." His smile broadened. "You know, the Word of God is profound, but it's not complicated. Mankind makes it complicated."

Annie thought it over but she wasn't sure. "And then what happens? After I'm saved?"

"Let's take one step at a time, Mrs. Fetherston."

"But how do I know that the Bible is really God's word?" she challenged him. "What about all the other religions in the world? My parents used to go to all different churches."

Dan smiled slow and easy. "Those are mighty good questions. But, you see, I'm not talking about a man-made religion. I'm talking about having a personal relationship with God Himself!"

Still smiling, he said, "The Bible tells us, in the Book of Acts, that when Paul and Silas preached to the Bereans, they received the word with all readiness of mind and then searched the Scriptures daily to see if all those things they heard were true." Dan gave her a pointed look. "Seems it's your turn to do a little searching. I mean, I could sit here and preach at you, but who am I and why should you listen to me?"

Annie was suddenly afraid that she had offended him. "Sorry. I shouldn't have—"

Dan held up a hand as if to forestall any further apologies. His expression was serious, but kind all the same. "Do you own a Bible, Mrs. Fetherston? This kind of Bible? The Holy Bible?"

Annie shook her head. "No, but I can probably get one at the library."

"Here, take mine," Dan said. "I've got another one, and I want you to have your own Bible. Then you've got it forever, no due dates. And you can search the Scriptures any time you want. . .even at 2 A.M.

"And let me suggest that you begin by reading the Book of John," he continued. "I think it'll answer some of your questions. But pray before you start reading and ask God to show you, in a way that only you can understand, that the Bible is truly His inspired Word. He will."

Annie smiled, but she was shaking her head at the offer. "I couldn't possibly take your Bible. I mean, it's your personal possession."

"It's a personal treasure. But I insist. Take it."

"Thank you, but—"

"But what? Do you have a problem accepting gifts or something?"

Annie understood his question's underlying meaning. However, instead of seeing mockery or arrogance in Dan's expression, as she had expected, Annie saw sincerity.

Then he smiled and gave her a friendly wink. "The Book of John. . .and remember to pray before you begin reading."

Annie nodded in resignation. "Thank you, Mr.—Mr. Brenshaw."

"Call me Dan," he told her. "All my friends do."

With that he walked away, leaving Annie holding the smooth, black, leather-bound book.

six

After everyone had finished eating pizza, the tables were cleared, and then Dan Brenshaw took the floor. He offered up a challenge to the teens and parents alike. He asked the people to open their Bibles to Psalm 101. From there he read, "I will set no wicked thing before mine eyes."

With an earnest expression, Dan asked everyone to search their heart. If they found that they had set wickedness before their eyes, both willingly and unwillingly, Dan encouraged them to confess it to the Lord and ask for forgiveness. Then he shared some of his own struggles.

Annie found that, as she listened, she came to appreciate Dan's open concern as well as his honesty to admit his own shortcomings. And that quality about him invited her to examine her own heart.

The challenge ended then, and the Winstons rounded up their children while Annie looked for Josh. He had spotted some friends from school and they had sat together up in front. Now Annie found Josh and three of his friends engaged in a lively conversation with Dan.

"It's the big football game next Saturday—a week and a half away," he was telling the boys. "Rain or shine. And, if it's raining, there'll be tons of mud."

"Aw, cool!" one of the boys exclaimed.

"Football in the rain is awesome!" Josh agreed, causing Annie to cringe inwardly. Football in the rain, in her opinion, made for an "awesome" mess!

Dan suddenly noticed her standing there and grinned. "Now, boys," he advised mischievously, "don't let your mothers hear you mention the words rain and football together in the same sentence. . .and especially don't say the word M-U-D around them, otherwise there could be trouble!"

Josh shot a wondering glance at Annie.

"Sorry, kid," she told him, "but I already heard the words

rain and football and M-U-D." She looked at Dan. "Sounds like a lot of L-A-U-N-D-R-Y for me!"

Dan laughed. "Oh, I sure am glad that you've got a sense of humor. For a moment there, I thought I was in hot water."

Annie lifted an impish brow. "You still might be, Mr. Brenshaw. The football game isn't till next week."

He sobered. "It's Dan, remember?"

Annie smiled slightly, feeling a little embarrassed at the reminder. "Okay, Dan. But then you'll have to call me Annie."

"It's a deal."

Annie's smile broadened as she tugged on the hood of Josh's purple sweatshirt. "Time to go."

"Glad you came, Josh," Dan said. Then he nodded the same to Annie.

Turning, she caught his gaze and smiled. Dan smiled right back.

"Oh, and. . .Annie," he said, as if trying out her name, "I hope you'll allow Josh to play football with us in a week."

Annie looked at Josh who was nodding vigorously. "Sure, okay, he can play."

A round of cheers broke out, and Annie laughed softly. But then, looking toward the door, she saw the Winstons waiting to leave so she hustled Josh away from his friends.

Fifteen minutes later, they were being deposited in front of their house.

"Glad you came, Annie," John said.

"We'll see you tomorrow at the store," Maggy added. "Bye, Josh."

Annie thanked them and elbowed a reminder to Josh.

"Thanks, Mr. and Mrs. Winston," he said on cue.

At the front door, Annie turned the key and they entered. The screeching, explosive noise that Stephen called music assaulted them at once. Even Josh grimaced.

"He's the one who needs church, Mom. Why don't you make him go?"

Annie didn't reply. She couldn't. The time for "making" Stephen do anything had long passed. And how could she explain that to Josh without giving him the same ideas? What if he decided to follow in his big brother's footsteps?

By this time Josh had run up the steps and, without knocking, entered Stephen's bedroom. "Turn it down, you jerk!" he yelled.

Annie heard Stephen mutter something obscene, after which Josh slammed the door on his brother. The volume of the stereo did go down, however, much to Annie's relief.

Feeling suddenly exhausted, Annie collapsed onto the couch, coat and all. She leaned her head back and became aware that she still clutched Dan Brenshaw's Bible. Rolling her head to the side, Annie gazed at its shiny, black leather cover. She had briefly flipped through it earlier tonight and noticed several underlined passages. There were a few scribbled notes on the sides of some of the delicate pages, too. This was obviously a very personal item, so why had Dan given it to her?

Lifting the Bible, Annie turned to the Book of John. Maggy had marked it for her with enthusiasm fairly oozing from every pore. "In the beginning was the Word, and the Word was with God, and the Word was God."

Annie paused, remembering that Dan had asked her to pray first.

"God?" she whispered, "if this Bible is really Your inspired Word, just as the Winstons and Dan Brenshaw claim, please show me in a way I'll understand."

With that, Annie continued reading. Too tired to get up and take off her coat, she stayed just as she was. Her curiosity kept her reading. Annie went right into the second chapter. And then the third.

She read about the man named Nicodemus, a "ruler of the Jews," and Annie realized that he was asking Jesus, almost two thousand years ago, the same thing that she was asking Him today: "How can a man be born again when he is old?" And, what's "born again"?

Annie kept reading, trying to understand. Then, on the bottom of the page, she read Dan's additional notes: "Jesus was saying: 1. you are a sinner; 2. you cannot earn a home in heaven—you need to trust Jesus only for salvation; 3. you must "call" on Him to save you."

Oh, yeah, she thought, *those three things that God wants me to know. . .just like Dan told me tonight. And, after I ask*

Jesus to save me, I'm born again. Annie smiled and nodded. *Okay, I get it.*

Stephen bounded down the steps, then stopped short when he spied his mother on the couch.

"What are you reading?" he demanded in a dark tone of voice. Then, before Annie could reply, Stephen fairly shouted, "You're reading a Bible! I don't believe it! Josh said you went to some church thing tonight, and now you're reading a Bible!"

Annie looked up briefly, but long enough to give her son a quizzical frown. "Stephen, I read a lot of things."

"But never the Bible!" He seemed genuinely agitated. "You know?" he added. "Something weird is going on in this house. I can feel it, man!"

Annie sighed wearily. "The only thing weird in this house is that stuff you think is music, Stephen." She looked back down at the Bible then.

"Stop it!" Stephen shouted, louder now. Then, in two great strides, he reached Annie and grabbed the book away from her. Turning, he threw it across the room.

"Stephen!" Annie cried with wide, horrified eyes. She looked at the Bible where it lay in a heap by the front door. "That was a gift!"

"Then give it back. Fast! I ain't livin' with no religious fanatics!"

"Listen here," she retorted, pointing a finger at him as if in warning, "this is my house, and if I want to read the Bible, I will!"

Stephen clenched his jaw, its muscle working inside his cheek. "Then maybe it's time I move out of your house," he told her sarcastically.

Annie was in no mood to be baited or threatened. She knew that if Stephen was going to move out, she couldn't stop him.

Without a word in reply, she walked over and picked up the Bible. It hurt her to see its pages wrinkled from Stephen's carelessness, and she tried to smooth them down into place.

Looking at Stephen then, Annie was shocked to see his face reddened with anger. For some odd reason it reminded Annie of a sorry cartoon with steam billowing from his ears—

Stephen looked as if he were about to blow.

She smiled gently in an effort to calm him down. "Stephen," she said lightly, trying to appeal to his common sense, "it's a Bible. That's all. I'm reading it. So what?"

In the next moment, Stephen erupted. He threw the magazines and newspapers off the coffee table in one great sweep of his arms. Then he kicked over the table, causing Annie to jump aside. Turning, Stephen grabbed a lamp and threw it across the room.

"What's wrong with you?" Annie cried, feeling frightened by her son's violent behavior.

But Stephen never seemed to hear the question and continued to furiously overturn tables and throw objects, many of which smashed upon impact. He emptied Annie's small bookshelf, throwing books everywhere in a wild rampage while she cried for him to stop. He pulled out the desk drawers and sent them flying, one hitting a framed picture and shattering its glass.

Then, finally, when all the damage was done and nothing appeared to be left unscathed, Stephen suddenly stopped. Annie, on the other hand, felt hysteria rising. *What happened to cause Stephen to go. . .go crazy?* she wondered.

She considered him at length, out of breath from his outburst, and she was afraid of him. She had no idea what he would do next. Their eyes met in a silent stand-off. Then Stephen said, "I hate you!" before he grabbed his coat and left the house.

Immediate tears pooled in Annie's eyes, but she couldn't deny the sense of relief she felt, too. So many times she had tried to stop Stephen from leaving, but tonight she was glad to see him go.

Josh appeared, looking ashen. "He's nuts," he said of Stephen.

Annie wondered about the truth of that statement as she surveyed the demolished living room. But what had set him off?

Wiping her tears away with shaky fingers, Annie looked at the Bible. She had been hanging onto it like a shield throughout the ordeal.

Then suddenly Annie looked over at Josh as a kind of understanding passed through her. "The Bible is real," she said decidedly. "It's really God's Word. I think He showed me that just now with what happened with Stephen. It's hard for me to put it into words exactly, but no other book would have affected a person like the Bible affected Stephen tonight."

Josh nodded. Then he righted a table and picked up a lamp.

&

The next day at work, Annie relayed the evening's events to Maggy when things were quiet in the store.

"Oh, I'm so sorry, Annie," Maggy said sympathetically.

"Stephen said he hated me, and he was gone all night."

Maggy shook her head, looking sorrowful.

"I wish things were different," Annie added, "but in the frame of mind he was in, I'm kind of relieved that he didn't come back home last night."

"I imagine you are."

Annie shrugged, feeling embarrassed by her relief at Stephen's disappearance but glad for Maggy's sympathy, too. "There is some good that came out of it."

"What's that, Annie?"

"Well, I believe the Bible is real. I believe it is really God's inspired Word now."

Maggy smiled.

"I read the entire Book of John last night and it was an amazing thing, but it helped my nerves. And I enjoyed reading about Jesus. I believe He is God's only begotten Son like the Bible says. Everything you've been telling me for months just suddenly made sense somehow. And I understand that I have to be born again to have eternal life." Annie paused, wearing a little frown. "Do you think you could help me, Maggy? I mean, I don't really know what I'm supposed to do."

"You just go to God in prayer, Annie. I'd love to help you." Maggy was smiling so broadly that tears shone in her eyes. "It's very easy. Let's go right now."

Annie nodded. Then she locked her register and followed Maggy to the office.

seven

Dan shook hands with John Winston as they met in the vestibule of the church that following Sunday morning.

"She got saved!" John exclaimed with a happy chuckle.

Dan smiled. "Amen! Who are we talking about?"

John laughed. "Oh, sorry. I guess I should have clarified that. I'm talking about Annie Fetherston. She accepted the Lord on Thursday."

"Is that right?" Dan was still smiling. He had seen hundreds come to Christ, but he never got tired of hearing of yet one more who entered into the Kingdom of God. "That's great, John. Is she coming to church this morning, too?"

John nodded. "Maggy and I took two separate cars so I could bring the girls and get here in time for the workers' meeting and so Maggy could pick up Annie and her son Josh."

Dan smiled, listening as he picked some Sunday School material off the central information desk. All church workers met at eight o'clock on Sunday to discuss the topics of that morning's Bible lesson. Dan and John both taught classes in the youth group.

"Is she going to attend a Bible study this morning?" Dan asked, referring to Annie once more.

Again, John nodded. "She's going to sit in with Maggy."

"Good."

"Yep. But there's bad news, too. Her sixteen-year-old son apparently left the house in a rage on Wednesday night and hasn't been home since." John paused, wearing a rueful expression. Then he lowered his voice. "Annie had to call the police Friday morning and report him missing. She hated to do it, too. She was hoping Stephen would come home on his own and that she would be able to talk some sense into him."

"Hmm." Dan replied, growing suddenly pensive. Then both men walked down the hallway, pausing just outside their respective classrooms.

"I think Annie is carrying around a lot of guilt," John stated.

"Probably so," Dan agreed. And then he was remembering his own mother and how she had fretted herself over his rebellious behavior.

When Dan was seventeen years old, he thought he ruled the world. That was back in 1977, and he, like Stephen Fetherston today, was chomping at the bit—wanting to go his own way. Dan had thought he was invincible; however, the path he chose back then was one of self-destruction. Dan only hoped that Stephen wouldn't have to learn the hard way, as he had.

"Does Annie know where her son is now?" Dan had to ask.

John shook his head. "No. And the police don't have any clues. Stephen hasn't shown up for school in days and is apparently hanging out with some older boys who have already dropped out."

"That's a shame," Dan replied. "I'll pray for him."

But then it was time for the workers' meeting to start. However, throughout its entirety, and then during Bible study time, Dan couldn't shake the feeling that God was calling him to help this family.

I'd help the boy in a minute. . .but Annie's a widow, Lord, he silently prayed an hour later as he made his way back to the auditorium and then over to the piano. *Couldn't the Winstons better handle this? Maybe I shouldn't get involved. . .I mean, I'm leaving in January!*

As his fingers touched the piano keys, Dan began to play a melody that he had composed. He played it now from memory as he allowed his gaze to wander around the auditorium. He watched as folks entered, found a seat, and conversed amicably. This was merely background music in preparation for the worship service that would begin in five minutes. Dan thought he could play background music in his sleep if he had to.

Then suddenly his gaze found Annie Fetherston as she walked up the aisle and took a seat next to Maggy Winston. Dan's first thought was that she looked real pretty in that green dress—

Dan halted his thought process, but then decided, *More's the reason I ought not get involved. Annie's a nice-looking woman, and this could be dangerous!*

Dan glanced her way again, as if he couldn't help it, and then Annie suddenly looked over at him. Their eyes met. Dan, in all his chagrin, managed to nod a slight greeting, but Annie smiled back at him, unabashed.

Very dangerous! Dan decided again, quickly looking down at the piano keys. Of course, he reasoned, *Annie could have been smiling at something Maggy had said. . .and she could have just happened to be looking my way. . .*

In the next moment, Dan was amazed at how the thought disappointed him.

Very, very dangerous! he concluded inwardly. *I had better just mind my Ps and Qs! Somebody else will just have to help the Fetherstons.*

The pastor stepped up to the pulpit as Dan made his way to a pew. Ironically, the message today was on love. Agape love. The kind of love that meant sacrifice, and Dan began to squirm. He felt as if God was speaking to him through Pastor Ashford—through the Word. Dan didn't want to involve himself with the Fetherstons or any other family in this church. He was leaving and the less ties the better—except he could never say no to God.

All right, Lord, he silently prayed, *show me clearly what You'd have me to do. I'm a bit thickheaded, as You know. . .*

As if in reply, Pastor Ashford said, "And if we really love the Lord Jesus with all our hearts, souls, and minds, loving one another and bearing one another's burdens should be an easy task. When the Lord calls us to love someone, it's because He wants His love to shine through us. We are but vessels. We go where the Lord wants us to go because we are His and we love Him. You see, it's not what we want, but what God wants."

Then, for the invitation, Pastor Ashford requested that Dan play the hymn "So Send I You."

Yeah, okay, Lord, Dan thought as he made his way up to the piano. *You don't have to hit me over the head with a brick!*

❧

Dan had accepted a Sunday dinner invitation to the Winstons' days ago and he thought he should have been surprised when Annie Fetherston showed up with her son Josh. But, considering what was on his heart lately, he wasn't. In fact, he had surrendered his all to God right after the worship service this morning. Dan decided he would help Annie with her eldest son—and her younger one, too, if that's what God wanted. And, if and when he did help her, Dan decided he would be a gentleman. His manners would be impeccable. But at the same time, he would be laid back and casual with Annie, so as not to make her uncomfortable. But he would distance himself, not in an uncaring fashion, but in an unemotional one. And he was all prepared, or so he thought, when Annie walked into the living room.

"Well, hi, Annie," he said lightly.

She was the one who seemed surprised, but only momentarily. "Oh, hi, Dan. I didn't know you were going to be here." She smiled. "It might have been easier getting Josh to come if I had known it."

"Really? How's that?"

Annie shrugged, then looked over her shoulder at the two ladies in the kitchen area. Maggy and old Mrs. Engstrom, whom the Winstons invited to dinner every Sunday, were chatting up a storm.

"Josh said he didn't want to spend his Sunday afternoon around a bunch of old ladies." Annie rolled her eyes. "I guess he's lumped Maggy and me into that same pot. . .of 'old ladies'."

Throwing his head back, Dan laughed. "I don't guess I want to hear what he thinks of John and me. . .old fuddy-duddies, perhaps."

"Oh no," Annie said, looking sincere. "Josh thinks you and John are the greatest. In fact, he's sitting in the family room with John right now, watching the Green Bay Packers on TV." Then she raised her brow and gave him a pointed look. "It was the talk about that football game in M-U-D that won him. Josh loves football—any sport, really."

Dan grinned.

There was a moment's pause as Annie settled herself onto the sofa. Dan continued to stand over by the desk and bookshelf where he had been snooping—with John's permission—at the Winstons' collection of literature.

"Any news on your oldest son?" When Annie looked up at

him, surprised, Dan explained, "John filled me in. I hope you don't take offense to that, Annie. We're both concerned. That's all."

She shrugged, then shook her head. "I'm not offended and, no, there isn't any news. I'm wondering if Stephen is even still in town. One of the teachers at the high school said there was a big rock and roll concert in Minneapolis, and she was certain those teens not in school on Friday had skipped out to go see it."

"Quite likely," Dan replied thoughtfully.

"The police haven't been able to locate him. One officer told me Stephen went underground." Annie looked over at Dan with pleading eyes. "What's that supposed to mean?"

"You didn't ask the officer?"

"No. I was too dumbfounded to ask," Annie replied, sounding disappointed with herself. "When the policeman said 'underground,' I had this vision of Stephen living in some awful burrow."

"Aw, c'mon, Annie," Dan said with a laugh. Even she had to chuckle.

"All right. I know what it means when someone goes underground," she confessed at last. "It's just that I can't believe that my son is affiliated with people who would willingly hide him from his mother, teachers, and the law."

Dan considered her. *She's very naive,* he thought. *Someone ought to be protecting her, looking out for her.*

"Annie, don't you have family around here? A father, brother, uncle. . .a man who could lend a firm hand to those boys?"

Annie shook her head. "I have one older sister who lives in England with her husband. He's in the military. And Eric's family lives in Kansas. I had thought about going to them after Eric died," she confided. "But, well, Eric didn't have a close relationship with his parents, and they never accepted the boys and me."

Annie stood. "I'm really okay," she said with a stubborn tilt to her chin. "I'll handle this situation with Stephen like I've handled everything else—I just give it my best shot and hope it all works out. I don't need a father, uncle, or brother. . .or any man, I guess."

"You need the Lord, though."

Annie smiled and gave him a nod. "Yeah," she murmured. "I need the Lord. I can see that now." Her smile broadened then. "And I made a decision this morning."

"You, too, huh?" Dan replied, grinning to match her smile. "I think many decisions were made this morning."

Annie lifted a puzzled brow, but Dan waved off any questions and encouraged her to continue.

"This morning's message was very different from last week's message," Annie commented.

"Well, you're very different this week, Annie." Dan gave her an easy smile. "So what did you decide this morning?"

Annie paused, as if collecting her thoughts. "I decided I have to love Stephen regardless of what he's doing," she stated at last. "You see, a couple of days ago, I thought I'd change all the locks in the house and disown the kid. After all, the last thing he told me was that he hated me."

Dan's heart felt a familiar prick. Hadn't he said that to his mother once? Hadn't she forgiven him? Hadn't she shown him the love of Christ? Was it his turn, now? With Annie?

Dan thought he could answer yes to all of the above. How he was to show the love of Christ to Annie was yet to be discerned.

"But I realized this morning," Annie continued, "that Stephen is like the Prodigal Son, like that story Jesus told."

Dan was smiling in utter amazement. "You've read the Prodigal Son, Annie?" He chuckled in disbelief. "I just gave you that Bible four days ago!"

Annie looked somewhat embarrassed. "Maggy and I discussed the Prodigal Son in Bible study today."

"I see."

"But I did finish the Book of John on Wednesday night. Then, over the last three days, I read the Book of Matthew." She smiled shyly. "I like to read. And I. . .I want to know about Jesus, so I've been reading the Bible every chance I get."

"Well, I'm impressed," Dan told her honestly. *This woman is going to take off like a shot!* he decided.

"You know what bothers me, though?" Annie said in a way that made Dan feel privileged to have her confidence.

"If everything in the Bible is true, which I've come to believe it is, and if a person must be born again, like Jesus said. . .then my husband. . .well, he wasn't. . .born again."

"Now, hold on, Annie," Dan stated quickly. "You can't judge another's eternal destiny. Only God knows a man's heart."

"But my parents, too—"

"You can't judge them, Annie, and I wouldn't even speculate if I were you."

"But—"

Dan held out a hand to forestall any further remark. "Don't, Annie. Don't torture yourself this way. Focus on the living, not the dead."

She was standing right before him now, and Dan saw tears cloud her large brown eyes. He felt like groaning—he was moved to compassion for her. Taking an unemotional stance wasn't going to be easy.

"Annie," he advised, "if you can't change it—not even through prayer—then you've got to give it over to God. And rejoice in the fact that our God is fair and just. Everyone gets a chance to make a decision for Christ."

She nodded and seemed to swallow her tears. Then she grew momentarily pensive. "Well, maybe I can't do anything to change the past," she said, with a sudden burst of determination, "but I can do something about Stephen, can't I?"

"That's right," Dan replied, growing more impressed with each word Annie spoke. "You can pray for Stephen. We'll all pray for Stephen." He paused, grinning mischievously. "Okay, here's a pop quiz for you, Annie. What does the Bible say about God answering prayers?"

Annie thought a good long moment. "I'm not sure."

"Think a minute longer," he said on an encouraging note. "Jesus said it in the Book of Matthew. He referred to it as being like the seed of something that tastes great on a hot dog!"

Annie looked at Dan like he was crazy—but then it clicked. "The mustard seed!"

"That's it!"

"Faith the size of a mustard seed. . .no, wait. It's smaller than that. Faith the size of a grain of mustard seed. . .then nothing will be impossible."

Dan chuckled. "You get an A-plus, Annie Fetherston!" Then she blushed profusely, making him wonder what he said to cause such a reaction.

"Well," she said at last, "I don't know about an A-plus. I need to learn how to pray. I'm not quite sure about it. . .and, about faith. Mine is microscopic and that's about all."

"And that's pretty good, Annie," Dan replied. "You're only a babe, four days old in Christ. I know a few Christians who have been believers for years and who don't have as much faith as you do."

"Really?"

"Really."

Annie smiled up into his eyes then, and Dan decided helping her might well be the hardest thing he had ever been called to do. She was charming and downright delightful! She had a desire to read her Bible and learn spiritual things, and Dan had to admit, he would like to encourage her along those lines. But, at the same time, there was something in the way she looked at him that caused Dan to feel a certain measure of alarm. He felt suddenly uncertain that his cautious decisions would withstand Annie's sometimes tearful, sometimes pleading, sometimes smiling brown eyes.

Maggy suddenly appeared at the living room doorway. "Dinner is served," she announced cheerfully.

Realizing his thoughts were leading him toward unwanted romantic feelings for Annie, Dan sighed in relief and headed for the dining room.

eight

Saturday morning, one week later, dawned a beautiful, sunny day with clear blue skies. The temperature, however, was all of thirty-five degrees. Dan telephoned each of the boys playing football that day, telling him to dress warmly. He also said the extra clothes would provide some padding against the cold, hard ground. . .when all of them took their turns hitting it!

&

Annie hadn't planned on going to the football game. But she had worked the early shift and got off at three o'clock, so she changed her mind. The game started at two, so Annie figured she could still catch some of it. She used to attend all of Stephen's little league games and swimming competitions. The least she could do was give Josh equal time.

Stephen. Annie still wondered where she went wrong with him. What hadn't she done? What hadn't she given him? Had she spoiled him somehow? Or deprived him in some way? Annie truly felt that if she had been a better mother to Stephen, he would be a better person today. Perhaps he would be home where he should be. But he had been gone all of a week and a half now, and Annie worried over him constantly.

She fought to squelch the guilty feelings rising within her now. What would it change to feel guilty? Nothing. And it won't change Stephen, she decided. However, she still had a chance to be a better mother to Josh.

After ringing out her cash register, Annie said good-bye to John and left the store. Then she walked over a mile to the football field where the game was still in progress.

Josh spotted her and waved right before he got tackled. Annie grimaced. *Why do they have to play so rough?* she wondered.

"Hi. Remember me?" a woman about Annie's age asked, coming up to her from the bleachers. "I'm in the Bible study with Maggy Winston, and I remember you visited last week."

Annie nodded and smiled.

"I'm Lisa Johnson," she said. "And you're Annie, right?"

"Right. You've got a very good memory."

Lisa shrugged, looking a bit embarrassed. "Not really. Maggy has had us praying for you for months!"

Annie's brows shot up in surprise. "Praying? For me?"

Lisa nodded. "For your salvation."

Annie turned away quickly, covering her sudden tears, and looked out over the football field. She marveled at the fact that the prayers of the members of Maggy's Bible study had come to pass.

It must work, Annie decided. Prayer. Praying and believing.

"Say, would you like to sit with us?" Lisa offered. "My husband, Craig, is over there." She pointed into the bleachers. "Some other mothers are sitting with us, too, and we've got hot coffee and popcorn."

"Sounds good," Annie replied, and she followed Lisa to the bleachers and then climbed up to a vacant spot.

The football game lasted another hour in which Annie watched Josh take one tackle after another. Is this really fun? she wondered. It sure didn't do much for her mother's protective heart!

"I'll be surprised if Josh doesn't have bruises covering his entire body," Annie commented to Lisa and her husband.

"And what about those men?" Craig asked, referring to Dan, John, and two others out there, playing right along with the kids. "I'll be surprised if they can move tomorrow!"

Annie chuckled at the remark. Then, once the game was over, she descended the bleachers with the Johnsons. On the field, the players had dispersed to the sidelines where parents could collect them and soothe their battered shoulders, elbows, knees, and, in some cases, egos.

Annie spotted Josh and walked over to him. "Nice game," she said with a smile. "Ready to go?"

Josh nodded. "But Mr. Brenshaw's giving me a ride home." With that, he threw his duffel bag over his shoulder.

Annie thought about the offer. "Well, I guess that's okay. Do you have your key?"

"Yep."

"Well, all right then. I'll see you at home."

"Okay, but don't forget I have my paper route," Josh reminded her.

Annie frowned. "Oh, that's right. . ." She paused, thinking it over. "Well, then, if I'm not home by the time you have to leave, be sure to lock up."

Josh nodded.

"See you later," Annie said with a smile before leaving the field.

"Okay, Mom."

Annie zipped up her jacket a little higher. Since the high school field was on the other side of town, Annie had quite a hike ahead of her. She didn't really mind it, though. Walking cleared her head. Besides, she was so numb already from sitting in the cold wind that she no longer felt its chilling bite.

Annie reached Acacia Lane and, preparing to cross the road, she heard someone call her name. Turning, she saw Dan Brenshaw jogging in her direction.

"Annie, hold on—"

She walked toward him, meeting him on the edge of the field.

"What's wrong?" she asked, frowning in concern.

"It's freezing cold out here and you can't walk home. That's what's wrong!"

Annie thought Dan seemed aggravated. His face was reddened by the wind and his blond hair was tousled. He wore an oversized green sweatshirt and black sweat pants and black leather cleats.

"Look, Dan, I always walk," Annie told him. "I'm seasoned, I guess. And if you think it's freezing cold now, just wait till January!"

Dan took her elbow. "I'm giving you a lift home, so don't argue with me," he said, half-pulling her back across the field. "And I talked to Josh about his bad manners. I hope you don't mind. But no boy ought to let his mother hike home by herself while he takes a ride."

Annie was taken aback by Dan's vehemence. She hadn't thought Josh was rude. She was accustomed to walking everywhere she went. How did Dan see this as some kind of injustice? Or, had Josh really been rude to her?

Maybe, she thought, *maybe I'm just used to having to persevere.* And if it were just her alone, Annie wouldn't have even thought of changing anything. But if Josh was really rude, and she didn't notice it, that was a problem; Annie didn't want her son treating others rudely!

๛

They finally reached Josh, and he looked at his mother with large, sorrowful brown eyes. "Sorry," he told her. "I should have made sure you had a safe way home, too."

Not to disappoint him, Annie gave Josh her sweetest smile. "Well, my mother used to tell me that when we stop learning, we're dead." She chuckled in hopes of relieving some of the tension. "Nice to know we're not dead yet, right, Josh?"

The boy rolled his eyes, but seemed to understand that he was forgiven. Dan's expression, however, was unreadable, and again Annie wondered what the problem was. Had she become an unwelcome tagalong? She quickly reminded herself that if she had, it wasn't by her choice!

"Okay, let's get our gear loaded up," Dan called to the four other boys standing around him. Josh made five and Annie, six. She wondered if there would be enough room in Dan's car. Maybe that's why he was wearing such a long face.

Annie caught his arm as the kids ran on ahead. "Look, Dan, I'm not a charity case."

He straightened to his full height. "Never said or thought you were."

"Then don't treat me like one. I get along just fine on my own. And nobody held a gun to your head and said you had to drive Josh and me home. We can walk. Josh is able and so am I." Annie paused and softened her tone. "But I appreciate your concern. . .and your offer."

Dan momentarily chewed the side of his lower lip as he considered her. Annie held her determined stance while looking him directly in the eyes.

"You're not obligated," she added. "And you seem a little edgy. . .so maybe it's better if. . .if Josh and I walk."

Annie opened her mouth to call for Josh, but Dan interrupted.

"Mrs. Fetherston," he said with extreme politeness, taking a step toward her while carrying a box of footballs in his arms, "it is my heart's desire to give you and Josh a ride home."

"Oh, cut the sarcasm!" Annie couldn't conceal the slight grin at Dan's tactics.

He just laughed, and Annie noticed that he had a "ha, ha, ha" kind of laugh and her grin grew into a broad smile.

"Aw, don't mind me, Annie," Dan said at last, sounding more like his old self. "I'm not edgy. I'm just sore all over. . . and we lost the game. I'm not a good loser. Never was. The Lord is just going to have to keep working on me in that area, I guess."

Annie couldn't help but drop her defenses at his honest admission.

Then she grinned impishly. "Well, if you think you're sore now, Dan Brenshaw, just wait until tomorrow when you can't move a muscle!"

"Yeah, yeah," he drawled, glancing at her from under a raised brow as they walked to the street.

Annie chuckled the whole way, deciding to take the ride after all.

They reached Dan's car, an old, blue Ford Fairmont, and the box of balls and duffel bags were loaded into the trunk.

"You four boys can squish into the backseat," he ordered. "And Josh, you can sit in the front, in the middle, next to your mom." Looking at Annie, he added, "The lady with the bad jokes."

She grinned, guilty as charged.

It took thirty minutes to drop off four kids, and when the backseat was finally empty, Dan said, "How 'bout we grab some burgers?"

Josh, of course, was all for the idea; but Annie hesitated, mentally counting the little bit of money she had in her purse.

Finally she acquiesced, but mostly because Josh's elbow of persuasion had gone into her ribs one too many times and now it was beginning to hurt. Furthering her rationalization, as Dan drove into the parking lot of the small mom-and-pop type diner, Annie decided that since Stephen had been gone, she had saved considerably on her grocery bill. She wished vehemently it wasn't so. But it was. And since it was, one night of fast food wouldn't break her financially.

Getting out of the car, Annie, Dan, and Josh walked into the diner, which Annie immediately recognized. It was a lonesome place, situated on the outskirts of town, and it had gone through several owners and various stages of popularity. Lately, however, it was just a hole-in-the-wall diner that consisted of five empty booths with orange padded seat cushions and a counter with eight matching stools. Some of the seats had been obviously repaired with cloth tape, and the worn chrome around the stools showed signs of age. But the tables seemed clean, and there were wonderful smells coming from the grill area behind the counter.

"Well, well. . .if it isn't Dan the piano man!" a big burly guy with a thick head of dark, curly hair cried. "Good to see ya!"

"Back at ya, Larry," Dan drawled with a broad smile.

The two men shook hands, and then Dan introduced Annie and Josh. Larry nodded a greeting to each of them.

"So what's on the menu tonight?" Dan asked.

"Well. . ." Larry grinned and appeared to be thinking about it as he wiped his hands on a badly stained white apron. "I guess I could fix up whatever you want."

Dan smiled, showing Annie and Josh to a booth. "Fix us up three of those mean hamburgers you're famous for. . .and three colas and three large plates of deep-fried onion rings."

"Coming right up," Larry said with a grin while Annie mentally calculated all the calories she was about to consume.

Oh, well, she thought with an inward shrug of resignation, *I'll start my diet on Monday.*

They got situated in the booth, Dan and Josh sitting across from Annie, and then Dan explained how he came to know about this burger joint and Larry.

"He was my friend when I didn't know a soul in Rhinelander," Dan began. "Mike and the rest of the evangelistic team had gone on to their next scheduled meeting, and I hung back to help Deerwood with its music department—the church and school both.

"So, I didn't know anyone well, except for Pastor Ashford, and I was only acquainted with him really. But, after the Hansons lent me their extra car—the very one we all rode in tonight, I happened upon this little diner that had no other name but the neon 'EAT' on the outside, and here I met Larry. He's a brother in Christ, though he doesn't attend Deerwood Bible Church." Dan grinned. "I, of course, am in the process of persuading him to join us. I mean, you can't beat the music at Deerwood Bible Church!"

Annie smiled and looked at Josh, who was eyeing an arcade race car game that stood in the corner of the diner.

Dan said, "This little place reminds me of a burger joint we had in Texas. Kind of helped me over my homesickness." He looked a bit embarrassed then. "After Mike and the rest of the team left town," he explained, "I felt pretty down and out for a few weeks."

Annie thought she could understand that. She had felt that "left behind" feeling when she quit high school to stay home and care for her dying mother. Her girlfriends, on the other hand, went on to their junior and senior years. Then, finally, they went to college. And though she wasn't angry or bitter over her past circumstances, Annie was saddened at times. She loved her mother deeply and it had been painful to watch her die. It had also been painful for Annie to lose her girl-friends as they moved on and she didn't.

Annie pulled her thoughts out of the past and turned her attention back to Dan. He must have suddenly noticed Josh's interest in the video game because he produced two quarters from his pants pocket. Sliding them across the table, he nodded toward the game. "Have fun," he said.

Josh grinned. "Thanks, Mr. Brenshaw." And then he was gone.

Dan chuckled under his breath. "It's an okay game, Annie," he assured her. "It's not violent or anything. I've played it several times myself. The cars go round and round and that's about it." He shrugged. "Although they do crash occasionally."

Annie considered Dan a moment. "I trust your judgment."

He looked up at her, seemingly surprised by her comment. Annie just smiled at him.

"You come highly recommended by the Winstons," she explained.

Dan lifted a mischievous brow. "As a piano player? Or

video game fanatic?"

Before Annie could reply, Larry appeared and deposited three tall glasses of cola on the table. "You guys want fried onions on those burgers?"

Dan and Annie both nodded.

"How about you, kid?" Larry asked Josh.

"Yeah, sure," he replied, sounding distracted.

The adults grinned.

Larry went back to the grill area, and Dan took a long drink of his cola.

"So, what do you do for kicks around here, Annie?"

She raised her brows in surprise. "Kicks? You mean, fun?"

"I do," Dan said, looking a little amused. "I guess traveling all over the United States I've picked up some unique verbiage."

"I suppose." Annie smiled slightly. "Well, I hate to disappoint you, Dan, but I don't do much 'kicking.' With two boys, a house to maintain, and a full-time job, I don't have much leisure time."

"I reckon you've got to make time, Annie. You can't just work, work, work."

She gave him a gracious smile.

"You're not one of those workaholics, are you?"

She laughed. "No. Not by choice, anyway."

Dan nodded and then looked over at Josh. Annie could sense that his mind was still on their conversation, and she had the feeling that Dan was going to delve a little deeper.

"Do you do a lot of dating?" he asked her abruptly.

Annie laughed softly. She couldn't help it. "I knew you were going to ask something like that."

Dan looked both embarrassed and relieved by her admission. "I hope I haven't insulted or offended you by asking that question. Believe me, that's not my intent. And you don't have to answer it, either. I'm just wondering what kind of a woman you are. . .or were before you got saved. And, not to judge you, Annie, but just to. . .to get to know you better." He frowned. "Am I making sense? I don't feel like I am."

"Back on the farm, we called that 'hoof-in-mouth disease'," Annie teased him.

Dan chuckled, looking chagrined. "Touché. I guess I have stuck my foot in my mouth."

"Well, to answer your question, Dan, and, yes, I'll answer it. . .I'm not offended, either. But, no, I don't do a lot of dating," she said in her most serious tone of voice. Annie had a point to make, and the sooner she made it the better. For both of them. The last thing she needed or wanted in her life was another person to worry about. Another mouth to feed. Another human being to take care of? No way! "I don't date at all, in fact," she continued, "so please don't ask me out because I'll just turn you down."

Dan nearly choked on his cola at that; it obviously hadn't been the reply he anticipated. Then, just as he caught his breath to explain what could only be his rightful intentions, Larry brought over the burgers and onion rings.

"Chow time," he announced.

nine

Annie noticed that Dan was very courteous the rest of the evening and he refrained from asking any more personal questions. Instead, he asked general things about Stephen and then steered the conversation over to Josh.

However, after driving them home and walking them to the front door, Dan held Annie back by her elbow. "Could I have a few words with you before you go inside?"

"Sure." Partially closing the front door, Annie stepped down onto the cement stoop.

"About before. . .in the restaurant. . ."

"Forget it, Dan."

"No, no. Let me finish. I'm sorry I got so personal. I just want to be a friend to your family. That's all. I was trying to think of some way to get to know you better. . .so I can help you with this trial with Stephen. It's Stephen with whom I think I might identify. . .because of my past."

"I understand," Annie said easily. "And I appreciate your wanting to help me. . .and Stephen."

Dan paused momentarily, as if weighing his next words carefully. "I'm not interested in you romantically, Annie, so you have nothing to fear from me. I'm leaving in January anyway, so I have no business courting you—or any woman."

Annie smiled at the word "courting." She hadn't known a man to say that since the last historical novel she'd read.

"I take it all's forgiven if you're smiling."

"Sure. All is forgiven." Annie even managed a soft chuckle, but only because she kept thinking of "courting." *What kind of man uses that word these days?* she wondered.

"Okay. Well, good night, Annie."

"Good night. . .and thanks for dinner tonight."

"My pleasure," Dan called from halfway down the front walk.

Annie entered the house, and turning and leaning against

the door frame, she watched Dan's retreating back. She suddenly found herself wondering what it would be like to be "courted." Oh, she had been dated before, but that seemed different somehow.

A man, a frequent patron at Paradigm Foods, recently asked Annie if she would like to spend an evening in a tavern, playing pool. Annie had declined politely—taverns and pool tables had never held much interest for her.

During the years she was a waitress, Annie had had offers for plenty of dates. However, many of the men asking had been drunkards or divorcees. Annie hadn't wanted to get mixed up in somebody else's messy affairs. She had her own mess to contend with—with Stephen and Josh!

And, as far as dating itself. . .well, Annie thought it seemed pointless. Another Saturday night, another date. And for what purpose? For kicks?

But courtship. Now, that was different. The term implied old-fashioned romance like the days of old-fashioned chivalry. When men were men and polite enough not to ask a woman into a tavern. When men were more like Dan Brenshaw, who held doors and chairs and picked up the tab for burgers and onion rings.

Annie Fetherston, she told herself, closing the front door and turning the lock, *you're a conservative farm girl who never finished high school. Dan Brenshaw is a scholar and an accomplished musician. And you can't even manage your two boys, the last thing you need is a man in your life! So what are you doing thinking of courtship with a man like Dan Brenshaw?*

❧

The next day, a bright, beautiful, fall morning, John Winston knotted his tie, then examined himself in the full-length bedroom mirror. After a final inspection, he nodded in satisfaction. Walking through the hallway and into the living room, John found Maggy. He smiled when she looked up from where she sat on the couch, sipping coffee and reading the Sunday newspaper.

"Breakfast is ready," she told him.

She moved to get up, but John stopped her. "I can serve myself."

In the kitchen, he found pans of scrambled eggs and sausages warming on the stove. Grabbing a plate, John began to help himself to generous amounts. He was ravenous this morning. *Must have been that football game yesterday afternoon,* he mused.

"There are blueberry muffins, too," Maggy said, coming up behind him.

"What's the matter? Don't you trust me in your kitchen?" John teased.

"I should say I don't," Maggy shot right back at him. Then she lifted a brow. "How do you feel? A little sore, perhaps?"

"Not a bit," John replied. However, by the look on Maggy's face, he could tell she didn't believe him. "Oh, all right. I'm sore. My legs, mostly."

"Poor baby," Maggy purred, sounding as though she was trying not to laugh. She didn't, but, instead, placed two large muffins on his plate.

"Where are the kids?" John asked as they walked over to the kitchen table together. He had suddenly realized that it was much too quiet in the house.

"I had the girls take Noah for a walk," Maggy explained, sitting down with him at the table. "It's such a lovely morning, but it's supposed to rain this afternoon. I figured the kids should get outside while they can."

"Good idea," John pronounced.

In reply, Maggy smiled her beautiful, gentle smile that he never tired of seeing. Then, as he prayed silently over his meal, she sipped her coffee.

Moments later, after two bites of eggs and half a sausage link, John asked, "Is Annie coming to church this morning?"

Maggy nodded. "I just phoned her, and she said that she and Josh would be waiting for me."

Maggy paused, looking thoughtful, which made John grow suddenly suspicious. After fifteen years of marriage, he knew when Maggy had something on her mind. And right now there was definitely something on her mind.

"Okay, spit it out," he said playfully.

"What? My coffee?"

"Oh, if it were only that, my dearest wife." John laughed.

"I know that look on your face. You're contemplating great world issues. . .or something."

"Or something is right," Maggy replied with a chuckle. Then she grew serious. "Annie told me that she and Josh went to dinner with Dan Brenshaw last night."

"Oh, yeah? That's nice."

"And then Dan phoned this morning and said he found some books on prayer that he wanted to share with Annie. He asked for her phone number, and I gave it to him."

"Well, good. Annie will like that."

"The books or Dan's phone call?" Maggy asked impishly.

John gave her a pointed look. "I don't know, but I was referring to the books."

Maggy smiled. "But that would be kind of nice, wouldn't it?"

"What? Dan and Annie?"

"Yes. Dan and Annie. If they fell in love, then Dan wouldn't leave in January." Maggy was all smiles.

John, however, lifted a challenging brow as he swallowed another bite of his eggs. "Or he could take Annie with him in January, and then we'd lose the best cashier we've got!"

"Oh. I hadn't thought of that."

John laughed. "Don't go playing matchmaker now, honey," he said lightly. "The last couple you did that to has yet to forgive us."

Maggy tossed her head in feigned indignity. "Well, I can pray about it. You can't stop me from doing that."

"And I wouldn't dare."

"But I did do something."

"Uh-oh." John bit the inside of his cheek to keep from smiling. He thought Maggy was the prettiest woman alive—even when she was playing matchmaker.

"I invited both Dan and Annie to dinner this afternoon. I mean, we had such a nice time last week," she added quickly.

John chuckled.

"They both accepted the invitation."

"Knowing the other was coming?"

"Well, no, but neither one knew the other was coming last week. They seem to like each other. Josh admires Dan—that much is obvious. Besides, they all went out to dinner last night."

John shook his head helplessly.

"And I just happened to mention to Dan that Annie really enjoys listening to his music in church."

John rolled his eyes. "Going for the flattery approach, huh?"

Maggy clucked her tongue. "I'll have you know that Annie really does enjoy Dan's music."

John shook his head again as he finished his breakfast.

"Well, anyway, Dan told me he would give Annie a couple of his recordings, along with the books on prayer."

"Sweetheart, I'm not at all comfortable with this," John said lightly, but firmly. "It sounds like you've been doing more than praying."

"Yes, but only this morning."

John frowned. "This morning?"

Maggy nodded. "I made two phone calls—to Annie and Dan."

"Good night, Maggy! You work quickly, don't you?"

She laughed softly and rose from the table and bent to kiss John's cheek. "I suppose I do," she replied in all honesty. "But that's all I'll do. I promise. I want the Lord to do the work—if there is even a work to be done between Dan and Annie." Maggy smiled. "So only prayers from now on."

John had to grin as he followed Maggy, who had taken his empty plate. He came up behind her and put his arms around her waist as she stood at the sink. Maggy's blond hair smelled as sweet as her personality, and in just that moment, he felt sorry for Dan, who had no wife. Even God said that it was not good for man to be alone.

"Tell you what, Maggy," he said with his chin on her shoulder as she rinsed the dishes. "I'll pray right along with you. I mean, maybe Dan does need wife—not that it has to be Annie, of course."

Maggy turned in his embrace. "And here I was thinking that Annie needed a husband. To help her with those boys. A man to protect her and provide for her like you do for me."

John smiled and kissed her nose. "Well, it goes both ways, honey. You take good care of me, too. But marriage isn't for everyone. Those who are single are very valuable to God in that they're free to witness anywhere He calls them. They don't have to be concerned with provisions for more than just themselves or packing up the babies and the homestead and relocating. There's a real sense of freedom in that, and it's one I know Dan treasures." John lifted a brow. "We have no right to meddle in what God has ordained."

Maggy shifted uncomfortably. "Yes, but—"

"But we can pray," John assured her. "We can pray, and if it is God's will, then maybe we will see a match between Dan and Annie. However, you and I, Maggy Winston, need to take care that we don't become busybodies."

Reluctantly, Maggy nodded.

❧

Two days later at the store, Maggy waved John over to the office. "I think something is going on," she whispered. Then she nodded toward Annie's aisle where Dan stood, checking out his groceries. "He always does his shopping on Mondays," Maggy said of Dan. "But here it is Tuesday, and he's doing his shopping today!"

John frowned. "So?"

"So, Monday is Annie's day off and here he is, shopping on Tuesday instead!"

John grinned, but shrugged. He wasn't really convinced it was anything at all. When Dan entered the store this afternoon, he had said he was thrilled at the way Annie had been devouring the books he had given her to read. She had finished one already. Dan said he spoke with Annie yesterday afternoon because she'd had some questions, but for the most part she was understanding the books. And best of all, Dan said those books on prayer referred Annie back to the Bible—like a personal, home Bible study!

"Maggy, I think Dan is just helping Annie grow in the Lord by providing her with information. That's all."

"But didn't you notice them talking on Sunday afternoon? It appeared to be a very heavy conversation."

"It was. They were talking about Annie's oldest son, Stephen," John replied. "Apparently, he stole her television on Saturday night while Annie and Josh were asleep. He crept into the house like a thief in the night. Literally! And Annie said she knows it was Stephen because he took all his music and the rest of his clothes." John shook his head. "Annie is amazed that she slept through it. Then, again, Stephen didn't exactly have to break in because he has a house key."

Maggy was nodding. "Annie told me the whole story this morning. But I didn't think Dan knew." She shook her head as if in wonder. "He must have been the first one Annie confided in."

"That doesn't mean anything. Dan is just trying to help. He suspects that Stephen is into drugs. Dan thinks it's the reason he stole the TV. It would also explain Stephen's irrational behavior a couple of weeks ago."

"Oh, dear. What does Annie say to that?"

John shrugged. "I guess she's having a hard time believing it. But it makes sense. In fact, the police side with Dan."

Maggy sighed. "Poor Annie. I know how she frets over that boy."

John nodded. He could tell that, like himself, his wife was truly burdened for the Fetherstons.

Just then Dan called a "See y'all later!" from several feet away.

John and Maggy waved their good-byes as Annie began to check out her next customer.

ten

Just after lunch on Friday, Dan entered Deerwood Academy's office to collect his phone messages. Janice, the secretary, handed him two. The first stated that his three o'clock piano student had canceled his lesson due to the flu. The second message was from the principal at Rhinelander's public junior high school. Looking up from the latter slip, Dan gave Janice a questioning frown.

"What does the principal from the junior high want? Did he say?"

Janice nodded. "It's something about picking up a boy who got suspended for fighting today."

Dan grinned patiently. "Well, now, I can see that much here on the message. I guess I'm wondering who did the fighting and why I'm supposed to do the picking up."

"I can't remember the boy's name," Janice muttered, looking embarrassed. "I think the principal said you were his next of kin. Apparently the school was unable to reach the boy's mother."

"Next of kin?" Dan had his brows raised in total surprise. Then he laughed. "No kin of mine lives on this side of the Mason-Dixon line!"

The secretary smiled. "Oh, well, I don't know. . ." Again, she looked embarrassed. "The principal called during a peak time, Dan. All four lines were ringing," she confessed. "I'm sorry I didn't get more accurate information."

"Aw, that's okay," he replied. Then with a sigh of resignation, Dan headed for the school office's door.

In the hallway, Dan weighed his options. He wasn't busy, so he could drive over to the junior high and check out the situation. On the other hand, he wasn't sure if he should get involved. Dan knew about twenty junior high boys—so which one got suspended for fighting?

Finally his curiosity got the best of him, and Dan decided to drive over to the other school. It would make him crazy all afternoon if he didn't; but he wasn't about to get wedged between parents and their children. He would side with the parents no matter what! No matter what this boy said, Dan wasn't going to shield his punishment. He wouldn't play defense lawyer; the kid would just have to accept the consequences.

His stance determined, Dan drove the short distance to the junior high and found it easily enough. Dan was feeling familiar with this town by now, having lived here for almost six months already. He knew most of the street names and thought he had a handle on the order of addresses.

Rhinelander was what Dan would call "a large small town." It had some ten thousand residents and many, it seemed, could size up a newcomer in thirty seconds. Most folks were tourist friendly, and yet a good majority seemed suspicious of anyone seeking citizenship, unless a man knew someone already established in town and could do a bit of name-dropping. Gaining the trust of these folks could be a harrowing business. During Dan's very first week here, someone told him that Rhinelander was like long grass—if you took a stick and stirred it around, a bunch of black snakes would crawl out. A fine welcome, indeed! However, Dan hadn't met any "black snakes"—at least not here in this town! Only good folks. Some were Bible-believing Christians, and others needed to accept the Lord Jesus Christ as their personal Savior. Dan was only able to lump people into those two categories: saved and lost.

The Wisconsin River ran right through the center of Rhinelander. It had a paper company and a logging museum. There were resorts scattered everywhere, and the fishing holes were plentiful. Dan had enjoyed living out the summer months here. The air was fresh and cool and the trees were tall and green. Patches of rolling, wooded hills were everywhere between town and highway, and now, being fall, the autumn colors were breathtakingly beautiful! Russet. Gold. Fire red. Orange. The trees on the hillsides seemed to flame against the day's blue, cloudless sky.

Dan parked his car on the street in front of the school. The building was a long, single-story structure. Inside, the main hallway had been set up to accommodate the lunch hour. Walking into the school's main office, Dan was unprepared for the sight that greeted him.

"Josh!"

The boy looked up, shamefaced. "Hi, Mr. Brenshaw." His nose had been bleeding—and profusely by the looks of it— for there was a large blood stain covering the front of his shirt. And Josh's left eye was so swollen, it was nearly shut.

"If you look that bad, what does the other guy look like?" Dan asked, shaking his head at Josh. Of all the kids he had thought might be in trouble, Josh Fetherston wasn't one of them!

Josh shrugged at Dan's question. "I guess the other guy is back in class," he said through swollen, bruised lips.

"Hmmm. . ." Dan frowned. "Okay, let me get this straight. You were fighting, got yourself pounded good, then suspended from school. . .but the other guy is back in class?"

Josh merely shrugged. "I guess so. I guess it was my fault."

Narrowing his gaze in contemplation, Dan thought something didn't sound quite right. Must be more to it. He'd have to get the facts before he made any assumptions.

Then, suddenly he had to grin at Josh. "You make a terrible punching bag, know that?"

"Yeah, well, I tried to fight back," Josh said defensively. "But there wasn't any time. One minute I was standing there and the next minute Dave Henderson's fists were all over my face!"

"So I see." Dan considered the boy more closely now. "Did the school nurse have a look at you yet?"

Josh shook his head.

"Did anyone give you an ice pack for the swelling?"

"No."

Dan shot a wondering glance at the school secretary who grew wide-eyed and said, "I'll get Mr. Baxter. I believe he's off the telephone now."

Nodding, Dan turned back to Josh. "So what happened?"

Josh squirmed for a moment before answering, "It's a long story. . ." His words trailed off, and there was a pleading look in his eyes.

Dan thought it over and decided to question Josh about the fight later. "You should have called your mom," he said at last.

Again, Josh gave him that look, as if begging him to take his side. "My mom is upset about Stephen. She found out this morning that he stole her jewelry, except she doesn't know when he did it. Could've been last week, or even the week before. We think it happened before he stole the TV. Anyway, Stephen took my mom's wedding ring that had a diamond on it and my grandmother's wedding ring, which was all gold, and my grandfather's antique watch and a silver bracelet."

Dan sighed, looking over at the other side of the office, now empty except for Josh and himself. He didn't know what to think.

"If I would've called Mom about this fight," Josh continued, "she would've had a nervous breakdown!"

Dan turned back to Josh and lifted a challenging brow. "And you think by calling me that you're going to hide this from your mother? Ha!" he said with a touch of sarcasm. "You should see your face! And you're right. It's enough to scare the best of us, let alone your own mother!"

"Mr. Brenshaw," Josh pleaded, "I can explain. See, I knew if I called you, you'd understand."

Before Dan could reply, Mr. Baxter, the school's principal, appeared. He was a tall, thin man with dark hair, graying on the sides. He wore a suit, minus the jacket for the moment, and his tie, with its multicolored triangles, stood out remarkably against the man's crisp, white dress shirt.

Dan signed the necessary papers, making sure Mr. Baxter understood that he was not any relation of the Fetherston family. The principal said that, under the circumstances, it was all right.

"I know Mrs. Fetherston, and I know she has to work outside the home. I'm already aware that Josh is willing to go with you, since he's the one who gave me your name. So if you're willing to take him, Mr. Brenshaw, I'll allow it."

Dan nodded. "I'll take him."

"Josh said you work at Deerwood Academy."

"That's right. I'm teaching music there this semester."

The principal nodded. "Well, then, I'm more than certain that it's safe for me to let Josh go with you." A tolerant smile curved his lips. "I am familiar with Deerwood's reputation."

"I hope that, in your estimation, it has a good one."

Mr. Baxter shrugged. "It's different, I guess. I'm not a religious man."

"That's good," Dan replied in all due respect. "Salvation is based on a personal relationship with Jesus Christ, not on man's religion."

Mr. Baxter didn't reply. In fact, he acted as though he hadn't heard a word that Dan just said.

"Oh yes. The length of Josh's suspension is four days," he announced, changing the subject back to the matter at hand. "Please inform Mrs. Fetherston of that."

"Yes, sir, I will. . .but, four days?" Dan frowned. "Is a suspension really necessary?"

"Mr. Brenshaw, when a child behaves in a violent manner—"

"A violent manner?" Dan was shocked. "Josh?"

"Mr. Brenshaw," Josh interrupted, coming to stand right beside him now, "I can explain. I can explain everything!"

Dan looked at Josh, then back at the principal. "Did Josh explain himself to you, Mr. Baxter?"

"Yes, he did. I heard his story and the other boy's as well." The principal paused, folding his wiry arms across his thin chest. "This is not Deerwood Bible Academy, Mr. Brenshaw. This is a public school and, clearly, the other boy's religious freedoms were being violated. In fact, that's what started the fight. Religion."

"I see." And at that moment, Dan thought he really did, too. Turning to Josh then, he said, "C'mon, buddy, let's go."

❧

Thirty minutes later, Dan was in the Fetherstons' home where he prepared an ice pack for Josh's battered nose. On further examination, Dan decided it wasn't broken. They could skip the emergency room this time. Dan was no doctor, but he had seen enough injured noses to know if one was broken or not.

In the living room, Josh planted himself on the couch with his ice pack, while Dan paced aimlessly, trying to figure out what to do. He realized then, and quite suddenly, too, that he was in the very place he had been determined to stay out of: He was wedged between a child and his parent.

"You should have called your mom," Dan told Josh. "I understand why you called me, but you still should have called her."

Josh pulled the ice pack off his face. "No, you don't understand!" he cried.

"Then, maybe you'd better enlighten me."

Josh paused, as if collecting his thoughts. Then he sighed heavily. "After Mom discovered her jewelry missing this morning," he began, "she sat down on the edge of her bed and cried and cried. I couldn't even make her stop. So that's when I promised not to turn out like Stephen, and I promised to be her best son and never make her cry the way he does." Josh looked close to tears. "And now this had to happen," he said, referring to the fight. "I couldn't call her! Don't you see?"

"Sure, I do, Josh," Dan told him with an understanding grin. "Take it easy, now."

Josh seemed to relax a little then, and he put the ice pack back on his nose. He grimaced as it made contact.

"Okay, so what time does your mom get off of work today?"

"She'll be home about a quarter to five."

"So she's off about four-thirty, huh?"

Josh nodded.

Sitting beside him on the couch then, Dan wondered what was the best way to handle this. He didn't think it would be such a great idea to thrust this whole thing on Annie. Perhaps she needed to be forewarned of Josh's appearance, particularly if she "cried and cried" this morning. No sense in having her cry and cry all night!

"Okay, this is what we'll do."

Josh sat up a little straighter, looking eager and interested.

"I'll leave my car here and walk over and get your mom at four-thirty. Then we'll go have coffee or something. . .if she's agreeable. But I'll do my best to persuade her. Then I'll explain what happened today."

"Yeah, that'd be great!"

"But you are by no means off the hook," Dan said firmly. "Understand?"

Josh nodded, looking humble.

"Now, suppose you tell me what happened today."

Josh settled back against the couch, still holding his ice pack. "Well, there's this kid at school named Dave Henderson, and he thinks he's real tough just 'cause he's in the eighth grade, but he hangs around with all the seventh graders because all the eighth graders don't like him."

Dan nodded and tried not to grin at Josh's rambling explanation. "Okay, I'm with you so far. Go on."

"So a bunch of us seventh graders were playing football at lunchtime when Dave comes over and starts pushing me and this other kid around. Then he starts swearing his head off, 'cause we wouldn't let him play. But we already had our teams from yesterday! And that's when I told Dave to quit swearing."

Dan frowned. "This boy was using bad language on the playground?"

Josh nodded. "Really bad language. Except none of the teachers heard him." He paused in recollection. "So, anyway, I told Dave that he was going to hell because God wouldn't let a sinner like him into heaven. And I told him that it was a real hell with fire, demons, and evil spirits. . .and I told him he was going there, so he started punching me."

"Oh, boy," Dan muttered, rubbing his hands over his face.

"So then a teacher came over, and Dave told her that I said he was going to hell. She thought that I was the one swearing, so I explained about hell to her, and she got mad and said that hell didn't exist—"

"Listen, buddy," Dan cut in, "I sure am glad you're saved and on your way to heaven. And I'm glad you know why you're saved. But you can't just tell folks that they're going to hell without showing them how they can be saved, too. Did you do that? Did you show Dave and your teacher how they could be saved?"

"Well. . .no. . ."

"And sometimes people are more receptive if you give them the gospel in a. . .a more positive way."

"But I didn't have time to be positive."

Dan smiled. "Then you must pray for a more opportune time, or give out a tract."

"A. . .a what?"

Dan stood and reached for his jacket, which he'd slung over the back of a chair. From the pocket he took out a small Bible and several tracts.

"This little pamphlet is called a Bible tract. It gives a brief explanation on how folks can know for sure that they're on their way to heaven."

Josh looked it over. "Cool! And I can just hand these out to people."

"Right."

"I can do that."

Dan smiled. "I knew you could." Then he opened his Bible. "Now, Josh, this book here is the apostle Paul's letter to the Romans. . .or just plain 'Romans' for short. Now, I'm going to teach you how to lead a soul to Christ, using the Bible. Tracts are nice for quick jobs, but the Bible is the best. The Bible is God's Holy Word, after all.

"Now, look here, Josh," he said. "This is what some folks call the 'Romans Road'."

Josh looked on with interest as Dan showed him Romans 3:23; 6:23; then back to chapter 5, verse 8; and finally Romans 10:13.

"That's how you can lead someone to the Lord using your Bible," Dan explained. "But if there is no time for that, you can give the person a tract. . .like in the case of Dave Henderson this afternoon."

"Yeah, a tract would have been better," Josh agreed.

"Might have saved your face," Dan added with a grin. "Okay, now I think we ought to pray for Dave. Let's ask God for another chance to witness to him. Let's pray for a better time and place."

"And my mom," Josh said. "Let's ask God to make it so she won't be too mad at me."

Dan smiled. "Okay, we'll pray for your mom, too."

Then, with heads lowered, Dan proceeded to pray, and Josh followed right along.

eleven

At four-thirty, Dan set out for Paradigm Foods. He had helped Josh with his paper route and then left his car parked on the street in front of Annie's house. Wearing his headphones and listening to a cassette tape in his Walkman, Dan walked the distance to the grocery store easily. He arrived just in time, too. Annie was getting off of work as he got there.

"Hi, Dan," she said cordially. She wore blue jeans and a pink and blue flowered sweater. She had just a hint of make-up on, and he thought she might just be the prettiest cashier in the place.

And then it bothered him that he had even taken note of such a thing. . .again. He couldn't afford to give his emotions free rein; he was here in Rhinelander to do a job. That's it. And helping Annie Fetherston with her boys was merely part of that job. That's it. That's all!

Recovering his determination, Dan returned her greeting with a "Hey, Annie." He had taken off his headphones now and let them dangle around his neck. Then he stood in her line and watched as she began to ring out her cash register. "Say, listen, I've got to talk to you about something. How about we go have a bite to eat at that little restaurant right around the corner?"

Annie seemed surprised by the invitation.

"Don't worry," he assured her, "it's not a date or anything."

She gave him a little smile. "Well, if it's talking you want to do, could we do it later? How about on Sunday? I'm so tired I think I could sleep for two weeks!"

Dan afforded her a look of sympathy, but shook his head. "This won't wait, Annie. It's really important. And I told Josh that we'd bring him carryout."

"You've seen Josh?"

Sheepishly, Dan nodded.

Then, as Annie considered the offer, Dan tried to give her

his best "this is really important" look. It must have worked because she finally acquiesced.

"I just have to finish up here," she told him. "Then I'll be ready to go."

"Sure. I'm in no hurry."

Maggy suddenly appeared and chatted amicably while Annie's machine ticked and clicked, calculating the day's transactions. Then Maggy took the cash drawer.

"See you tomorrow, Annie."

Annie nodded.

"Bye, Dan."

"See ya, Maggy. Oh, and tell John that I'm planning to win the teen bowling party recruitment contest." He grinned at Annie. "Try to say that fast three times!"

She smiled.

Maggy said, "I'll relay your message, Dan, but you won't win this one. John has a plan this time."

"Yeah, sure," he teased with a wink at Annie. "I heard he had a plan last time, too."

Annie chuckled softly.

"Well, this time is different," Maggy replied. "I thought of this plan."

Dan feigned a worried look. "Uh-oh. I guess I'd better consider myself fairly warned, then."

Maggy laughed as she walked to the office. Annie grabbed her purse and then she and Dan left the store.

"Nice day," Dan remarked as they walked down the sidewalk. "I love the fall season in these parts."

Annie nodded in reply, and Dan thought she looked as tired as she had confessed to being. It's her eyes, he decided. They don't have their usual sparkle.

Finally she said, "I've been wondering if John and Maggy think we're. . .involved. Romantically, I mean."

Dan grinned. He couldn't help it. "Oh, yeah? How's that?"

"Well, every time you check out in my line, which is every time you come into the store these days, John and Maggy are always whispering and then they give me these funny looks." Annie shrugged. "I don't know. Maybe it's just my imagination."

"Want me to go through somebody else's line next time? I

just go through yours because I enjoy talking to you."

"No. That's okay. I like talking to you, too, and I guess I really don't care what John and Maggy think. I mean, it's not as if it's a bad thing they're thinking about us."

"No. It's not a bad thing."

"It's just inaccurate."

"Right. I mean, correct. . .your statement, that is. . ."

There was a moment's pause.

"Maybe you could talk to John," Annie suggested.

"Maybe you could talk to Maggy," Dan suggested right back. "It's usually the women who start this kind of stuff."

Annie laughed. "It is?"

"Well, sure. You're one. You should know."

"Yes, but I don't start stuff like this. I don't think Maggy does, either."

"Well, I'm glad to hear it," Dan said with a grin as he glanced in her direction.

Annie just shook her head at him. "And now we left the store together. . .you didn't even buy anything. This will look really suspicious to John and Maggy."

"Do you mind what they might think?" Dan asked, feeling curious as to what Annie thought about it all.

She shrugged. "I guess I don't."

Dan gave her a smile. "Well, listen, if the Winstons really have a problem with anything we're doing, they have a responsibility to speak to us about it. Okay? And, as someone who values his work in the ministry, I've gone to great lengths to make certain that our meetings are always in public or that Josh is along." He paused. "For propriety's sake—to forestall any gossip."

Annie nodded, looking grateful. "I appreciate your thoughtfulness, Dan. I suppose I'm just making a big deal out of nothing." She stopped, momentarily pensive. "But why couldn't we have talked at my house this evening? I mean, if Josh is there. . ."

"You'll see," Dan replied as they arrived at the restaurant.

He held the door open for Annie, and then they sat down in a booth by the window. The place wasn't crowded, as it was still early for the dinner hour.

"Okay, so what's going on?" Annie asked as soon as the

waitress deposited the menus and left to get them each a glass of water. "Is it Stephen? Did you learn something else about Stephen?"

Dan shook his head. "No, Annie, I didn't."

She leaned back in her seat, but it looked more like a collapse. "Did Josh tell you the latest?"

"About your jewelry? Yes, he told me."

Annie was thoughtful for a few long moments. "I was at the police station on my lunch break about my jewelry, and they mentioned the possibility of Stephen's involvement with drugs. That's not the first time the police have suggested that, as you know. Dan, do you think Stephen could really be into drugs?"

Dan pondered the question momentarily. "It sure seems that way, Annie."

"But maybe Stephen is stealing things from me in order to pay rent. . .or room and board."

"That would almost seem like he's trying to be responsible in a backwards sort of way." Dan glanced over the menu at her. "Do you honestly think that he's trying to pay his way somewhere?"

"I don't know."

"When I was sixteen, I had at least half a dozen hangouts where I could stay for free with friends who were as delinquent as I was."

Annie sighed audibly, a heartfelt sigh, and Dan felt compassion for her. He only wished he didn't have to tell her about Josh on top of it.

Remembering, then, that Josh had said his mom "cried and cried" this morning, Dan immediately took his headphones off from around his neck and laid them and the cassette player on the table. He didn't want Annie to cry and cry right here in the restaurant, so he decided to change the subject—at least momentarily.

"This isn't the greatest recording," he explained, pointing to the cassette inside the player, "but this piece isn't ready for a professional recording yet. It's my latest composition. I don't even have a title for it. Here," he said, pushing the headphones in her direction, "take a listen. Tell me what you think."

"Well. . .all right." Annie smiled and put on the headphones.

She listened quietly until the waitress came back, ready to take their orders. Both had selected the daily special: lasagna with a tossed salad and crusty Italian bread.

"So what do you think?" Dan asked about his music, after the waitress left.

Annie smiled, and this time it reached her eyes. "I liked it."

"What did you like about it?"

She looked embarrassed. "Well, this might sound silly, but I imagined the ending of a dramatic production while I listened to that melody."

"Oh, yeah?"

"Yeah. And it would be the kind of production that. . .that makes you laugh and cry throughout its entirety. And, at the end, the heroine emerges victorious over her adversities, but it's terribly bittersweet, of course, because she's lost so much. So you'd need a half a box of Kleenex just to survive the ending alone." Annie had been stirring her water with a teaspoon as she spoke, but suddenly she looked up at Dan. "And this piece of music would be the theme song—like the melody in the movie 'Driving Miss Daisy'."

"Hmmm. . .well, I'm flattered, Annie," Dan drawled, "that you think my music is comparable to the score of a major motion picture." He paused, then, in momentary thought. "So, is there a hero in this dramatic production of yours?" he asked before realizing how it would sound to Annie. Except he really wanted to know. Was she still in love with her husband, even though he was dead? Who did she see when she closed her eyes and listened to his music?

But Annie just shrugged, looking sort of dreamy. "I don't know about a hero," she said. "I didn't really think of specific characters or people. It was just the music, Dan. You're very talented."

"Thanks, Annie," he replied, a pleased smile curving his lips.

Then he reminded himself that he shouldn't care about whom Annie thought of when she closed her eyes. It was none of his business. He was leaving in January, and he was only helping her out. . .temporarily.

"Okay, so what's this very important thing that couldn't wait?" Annie asked.

Dan considered her for a long moment. Then he nodded. "I suppose I've procrastinated long enough, huh?"

Annie tipped her head to the side. "It's that bad?"

Dan didn't reply right away. Then, he said, "Josh was in a fight at school today."

Annie gasped.

"He took a good beating, but he's all right. He had the school call me because he was too ashamed to tell you. He said he had just promised to be your best son and all that."

Annie nodded ruefully. "He did."

"Well, apparently Josh attempted to witness to another boy who took offense and pounded him good. Of course, Josh didn't do such a great job at witnessing, but we talked, and I think he understands what he did wrong."

"All right." Annie sounded hesitant, as if she knew more was coming.

"Anyway, the fight was centered around what the principal called religion, so poor Josh is suspended for four days."

"Four days!"

Dan nodded. "I'm sorry to have to tell you that, Annie."

Annie couldn't believe what she was hearing. She nervously began to stir her water with a straw.

"When Stephen was in junior high," she began, "I begged that principal to help me. I wanted psychological testing for Stephen, but that man shrugged me off. He acted like he didn't have time for Stephen and me. It wasn't until Stephen was in high school and in real trouble that I was able to get some cooperation. . .but from the high school guidance counselor."

Annie looked over at Dan. "But Josh isn't nearly the problem Stephen was. . .and is. Oh, Josh gets into trouble, but it's boy stuff. It's not shoplifting or being an accomplice to auto theft. And I can usually reason with Josh where I couldn't with Stephen."

Annie sighed heavily, feeling discouraged. "After Eric died and I had to work, Stephen took advantage of the freedom he had—which wasn't my choice to give him. But there wasn't anyone to support us financially except me! I tried waitressing at night so I'd be around during the day, but instead of taking responsibility like I tried to encourage him to do, Stephen would sneak out of the house and leave Josh all alone. So I hired a babysitter—a college student. But she quit after two weeks because of Stephen's bad behavior. And that was okay, because I couldn't afford her anyway.

"Finally, I decided that I had to be home at night, so I got a job at the paper factory during the day. That worked out pretty well, even though Stephen skipped out of school a lot. But when summer came, Stephen had his days free and got into even more trouble. I tried to get jobs for him, like mowing lawns and farmhand chores, and I arranged a place for Stephen to stay so he wouldn't have to babysit for his younger brother, but it always seemed like Stephen chose the bad over the good. No matter what I did or how hard I tried."

"That's called rebellion, Annie," Dan told her. "And the Bible says that rebellion is the same as witchcraft. Little wonder Stephen is where he is today."

"And now Josh!"

"No, no, no. Josh is an entirely different creation altogether." Dan grinned. "The kid has got potential, Annie. I mean, any boy who takes a beating trying to share his faith in Christ has got potential!"

Annie found that hard to believe somehow. "Then why is Josh suspended?"

"Because, for Christians, this life is one big war zone filled with spiritual battles."

Annie thought a moment. "You're talking about spiritual warfare, aren't you? Like that section I read in one of those books you gave me on prayer. Is that it?"

"That's exactly it." Dan smiled, looking pleased. "And this sort of persecution is going to happen, because it's them against us."

"Oh, great," Annie said with a note of sarcasm.

Dan just chuckled. "But remember, we're on the winning side—except Satan doesn't want anybody else to know it, particularly Christians. He wants to cripple Christians so they can't go on for the Lord. Satan wants them to feel lost and discouraged."

"Well, he's doing a good job on me," Annie replied. "I feel like the worst mother in the whole world." Tears sprang into her eyes and an errant one slid down her cheek.

"No, Annie, you're not a terrible mother. Don't let Satan whisper those lies to you. See, that's not God's voice; He doesn't deal in accusations. God deals in conviction and then gives Christians the opportunity to repent. If we confess our sins, He is faithful and just to forgive our sins and cleanse us from all unrighteousness—and that's a promise right from the Bible! After that, we're free in His forgiveness. And God isn't anywhere in guilt and shame. Christ has made us free from all that."

"But I must have done something wrong," she choked.

"And maybe you did. Nobody's perfect. My mom wasn't perfect when I was a teenager, but I can't blame my rebellious decisions on her. And, from what I know of you, Annie, I'd say that you've done what you thought was right and acted out of love for your boys."

Annie managed a nod. She certainly had tried to do right by her kids.

The waitress appeared with their food, setting down their dishes. Then Dan prayed over their dinner, asking for God's blessings. Before they began to eat, Dan asked if Annie needed anything else. Annie shook her head and marveled at the extent of Dan's good manners. She suddenly found herself wishing that her boys would grow up to be just as caring and polite as Dan Brenshaw.

"What was your mom like when you were growing up?" Annie ventured. "Is she still alive?"

Dan nodded. "My mother is very patient and forgiving. She put up with a lot from me."

"But you turned out all right."

"By God's grace, yes."

"Then there's hope for my boys, isn't there?"

Dan chuckled. "Yes, there's hope, Annie, because there is a God and He is in control."

Annie nodded, and while they ate, Dan expressed his ideas concerning Josh. He told Annie there was "fruit" in her household and that, with the right kind of training and encouragement, Josh might go on for the Lord. A preacher. An evangelist. A teacher.

"Josh?" Annie could hardly imagine it.

"Annie, I believe you ought to forget the public school," Dan said boldly. "Public schools are fine for some. In fact, they can be veritable mission fields! But Josh is a new babe in Christ with a lot of growing to do. He could easily get sidetracked at the public school, so I think you ought to put him in Deerwood Academy."

"Oh, like right!" Annie replied tartly. "And where am I supposed to get the money for that? I can't afford a private school!"

"Yeah, I know. But that's where God comes in. He loves to prove Himself to new believers, Annie, and He wants to show you that He can take care of you and provide for you and your boys."

Annie didn't know what to say to that and several long, pensive moments passed. *Someone taking care of me?* she pondered incredulously. *And that someone being God Almighty?* Annie could scarcely fathom it! For most of her life, it seemed, she had been taking care of everyone else.

Then Dan encouraged her to talk to the principal of the Academy to find out about any available financial aid or scholarships. Annie agreed to at least that much. She'd love for Josh to go to the Academy. Its upstanding reputation around town was something other private schools vied to obtain. Annie had never bothered to consider the school for her sons—she couldn't afford the tuition. However, it couldn't hurt to get some information.

They finished eating and Dan paid for their meal and left the tip, gentleman that he was. Then they walked slowly back to Annie's house. When they arrived, Dan insisted on seeing Annie inside.

"You really don't have to do this," she said as they walked up her driveway to the side door."

"I know I don't have to," Dan replied. "I want to."

Annie felt flattered by his admission. More so, it made her feel special somehow. But she didn't want that; it would only make her grow fonder of Dan.

And I just don't need another person to take care of, she thought as she fished in her purse for her house keys. Finding them, Annie opened the side door, letting herself and Dan into the kitchen. *Besides, he's leaving in January,* she reminded herself. *So no more courtship ideas!* Annie had to smile, then, thinking of that word "courtship."

"Josh?" she called, setting down her purse on the kitchen table. The house was dark, save for the soft light that was on above the sink. "Josh?"

He stepped out of the shadows as Annie reached the living room. She yelped in surprise.

"What are you doing in the dark?"

Then, as Josh came forward, Annie turned on the central kitchen ceiling light. She gasped as she looked upon his bruised and swollen face.

"Oh, my. . .!" Annie couldn't even finish the exclamation, she was so horrified. She turned to Dan, eyes wide and disbelieving.

"I'm sorry, Annie," he said. "I tried to warn you."

"But you didn't tell me his face is so. . .so. . ."

A surge of anger suddenly filled Annie's entire being. She turned back to Josh. "Who did this to you? I want names. I'm calling some parents. No. . .in fact, I'm calling the police!"

Dan stepped forward then, coming to stand right behind her. "Calm down now, Annie."

She swung around to face him. "Look what they did to my son!" she cried.

"Mom, it was one kid," Josh tried to explain. "A big bully who thinks he's so tough just 'cause he's in eighth grade. And he weighs twice as much as me, otherwise, I wouldn't look this bad."

A rage Annie had never known before shook her from the inside out until she trembled with it. "I feel like doing to that kid just exactly what he's done to you, Josh!" she stated honestly and vehemently. Annie wasn't a violent person, and she knew she was speaking out of her emotions now. But she couldn't help it.

"Annie, the Lord says, 'Vengeance is mine,' " Dan told her softly. . .gently. "God says, 'I will repay.' "

She looked at him and struggled to understand what he was telling her.

"No one gets away with stuff like this," Dan explained. "Oh, it may seem like sin goes unpunished sometimes, but it doesn't. The boy who hurt Josh will reap the consequences of his actions someday, although we, as believers, would rather see him get saved than suffer the wrath of God." Dan smiled. "Right?"

"I don't know," Annie muttered. But, in her heart she knew that Dan was speaking the truth.

Then suddenly frustration and helplessness replaced all the anger Annie had felt only moments before and she broke down. She put her face into her hands and wept.

"Mom, don't cry," Josh begged, hugging her around the shoulders. He was nearly as tall as Annie, and she thought it ironic that she noticed such a thing at a time like this! "I'm sorry I got into a fight," Josh continued. "I'll do anything, Mom, only don't cry!"

"Come on, Annie," Dan said, "cheer up. We'll get Josh into the Academy. . .just like we talked about earlier."

"The Academy?" Josh pulled back from his mother and looked at Dan, his eyes round with surprise. "I don't want to go to school at the Academy. Those kids are a bunch of preppies!"

"Yeah, well, at least they're not allowed to fight and use bad language on the playground," Dan replied.

"Who was using bad language on the playground?" Annie said, sniffling.

"Dave Henderson. . .except the teacher thought it was me because I told Dave he was going to hell."

"Oh, Josh." Annie sighed heavily.

"But it's not really such a big deal," the boy continued. "And it sure doesn't mean I gotta change schools!"

Annie squared her shoulders. "Yes, it does. Mr. Brenshaw is right." Turning, she looked at Dan. "I'm going to check out the school on Monday morning."

Dan smiled.

twelve

Two days later, Annie was almost surprised to find herself sitting contentedly on the padded mauve pew. In the past, whenever Stephen or Josh got into trouble, feelings of guilt and shame lingered for days as Annie berated herself for being a bad mother. This time, however, she had good friends to help her through it. . .and this time she had God. Amazingly, Friday's incident with Josh seemed miles away.

Glancing around the auditorium, Annie looked on as the friendly people of Deerwood Bible Church laughed and talked in the aisles; however, Annie was more than happy to just sit and listen while Dan played the piano. At her request, he was playing the composition she'd heard at the restaurant on Friday. The melody deeply moved Annie, and she had so wanted to hear it again. Dan said he would play it for her, but then he teasingly added that, in return, she would have to help him think of a title. Annie said she would try.

Listening to the music, Annie turned her gaze toward the front of the church. The altar was decorated with pretty fall-colored flowers. There were only about one hundred members at Deerwood Bible but everyone, it seemed, took a personal interest in maintaining and decorating the church— and school, too. And Dan said both ministries were growing at a healthy rate due to Pastor Ashford's straightforward preaching from God's Word. Annie believed it, too, since she was experiencing that same growth herself.

Annie sighed, feeling fulfilled in a way she never dreamed possible. She was learning, stretching her mind, and it felt wonderful! Between her Bible study class on Sunday mornings and all the books Dan was giving her, Annie felt like she was back in school. Feeding her mind. Pondering on things of value—eternal value!

❧

The choir suddenly began to gather on the platform behind

the pulpit. Dan had finished playing his song and was now beginning a traditional hymn. Josh appeared, his face still badly bruised. Oddly enough, no one gaped, although several people had expressed concern this morning. Annie didn't really mind explaining, either, because most of the congregation here seemed to genuinely care about her and Josh. . .and Josh seemed to actually enjoy all the attention. Sliding over now, Annie made room for him on the end of the pew.

"Mom, guess what?" he began enthusiastically. "Mr. Brenshaw said there's going to be a bowling party next Saturday."

Annie smiled. "Yes, I think I heard something about it on Friday. Did you sign up?"

Josh shook his head. "Mr. Brenshaw said I should check with you first. But can I?"

Annie nodded. "I guess it's okay." Then she wondered how John and Maggy's recruitment plan was coming along.

"My punishment is over by Saturday, right?" Josh asked hopefully.

Annie nodded once more. "It ends Friday night."

"Whew!" Josh sighed. "I'll be ready for a little fun by then."

Annie had to smile, thinking of Josh's "punishment." It had actually been Dan's idea. He had come to her rescue again, and Annie realized that he seemed to do that quite often lately. As a friend, of course. Nothing more. And Annie truly appreciated Dan's friendship.

As for Josh's punishment, Dan had suggested that Josh ride along with him to school this week and work. Dan said the school needed floors scrubbed, carpets vacuumed, and the teen room needed painting—but first the walls had to be scrubbed down. Annie figured that Dan's method of punishment was the best way to deal with Josh, much to Josh's horror. However, he did admit that he liked the idea of going to work with Mr. Brenshaw for a whole week. Josh just didn't like the idea of all that work! Dan felt that, in addition to learning a good lesson through some hard work, being at the school for a week would help Josh get acquainted with his surroundings, and maybe he'd even meet some new friends. Then, the next week, Josh would start school there, right along with the new quarter.

Dan, Annie thought, was overconfident that things would work out. . .including the financial end of Josh's education at the Academy. However, Annie still believed that it was God's will for Josh to go to school here, and she was determined to keep her appointment tomorrow morning with Mr. Wells, the Academy's principal. She had spoken to him this morning, and he gave her a packet of information to review before their meeting. The packet contained the school's doctrinal statement, tuition amounts, and payment plans. Annie was a little afraid to look at it, but since she'd come this far already, she figured it wouldn't hurt, and she planned to study the packet tonight at home.

"I still have to do my paper route too, huh, Mom?" Josh asked now with a pained expression as they stood for the opening prayer.

Annie nodded. "Yes, you still have to do your paper route. And your usual chores around the house as well."

"Man," he sighed, "I'm going to be dead by the end of the week!"

"Yes, and I know the feeling well, Josh," Annie quipped. Then she grinned as she lowered her head to pray.

❧

It was getting to be a ritual—going to the Winstons' house for Sunday dinner after the worship service. But Annie enjoyed it. She liked the Winstons' company. And their daughters were charming and polite, though Josh said he disliked them. He called them "prissy" and said they couldn't catch a softball if their lives depended on it! Annie, however, thought the girls were everything little girls should be. Delicate, feminine, and each played the violin. And every Sunday, after dinner, they played for the house guests. Josh hated it, of course, although he said the piano would be okay if he had to learn an instrument.

Annie smiled now, as she sat at the dining room table with old Mrs. Engstrom, who talked up a lather! Annie felt a little guilty that her mind had wandered off, but she had heard this same story last week!

From where she sat, Annie could hear the men talk as they

watched the football game. Josh, Dan, and John occupied the den every week while the ladies listened politely to Mrs. Engstrom chatter away about her eighty-three years of life. And, while much of what Mrs. Engstrom had to say was very interesting, Annie thought she would much rather be in the family room watching the Green Bay Packers with the guys. She decided that she wouldn't be welcome, though it was an unspoken thing. But Annie could sense it. The men needed to be able to act like men. They reclined on the sofa and matching armchairs and kicked off their good leather shoes. An occasional belch could be heard, and Annie knew it was Josh. But she also knew that he would be reckoned with, and she felt Josh needed to be in the company of good men like Dan Brenshaw and John Winston.

"So, did you get to look at the information from the Academy?" Maggy asked, getting a word in quickly after Mrs. Engstrom began to wind down.

Annie shook her head, but she had the packet right there and opened it up. "I'm a little afraid to look at the tuition cost," she admitted.

"Let me take a look at that," Mrs. Engstrom said authoritatively. "I used to be a schoolteacher, you know."

Annie and Maggy exchanged a wondering glance, but Annie handed over the material. Then Annie explained the circumstances behind her desire to see Josh in the Academy.

"Yes, I saw his face, that poor, dear child!" Mrs. Engstrom exclaimed, looking over some of the papers.

"But it's not just the fight last Friday," Annie continued, and she spoke of Stephen and how she wished she would have known the Lord when Stephen was Josh's age. Or even before that—Annie wished she would have been saved while her husband was still alive.

"Well, you know what Jesus says about dwelling on the past," Mrs. Engstrom replied. "He says, 'No man, having put his hand to the plow, and looking back, is fit for the kingdom of God.' " The old woman paused. "The past is just that. . .the past. You can't change it. You can only accept it. . .and pass it on to others so they can learn from your mistakes."

Annie pondered the idea. Hadn't Dan once told her something along those same lines? "Where does Jesus say that?" she asked. "About not looking back?"

Mrs. Engstrom had to stop and think, while Maggy grabbed her Bible off the counter and began searching.

"I believe it's in Luke," Mrs. Engstrom said.

Minutes later, Maggy confirmed it. Luke 9:62. Annie wrote it down. She wanted to look it up for herself. Later. She enjoyed looking up specific passages in her Bible and then applying them to her life. It was as if a whole new world had been opened to her, giving her a sense of hope like she had never experienced before.

"But I can say I know how you feel," Mrs. Engstrom said of Annie's concern for Stephen and Josh. "I lost my two sons in the Korean War. My husband, Hank, rest his soul, convinced them that it was their duty to go. . .to serve their country. And it was. But neither Hank nor I knew the Lord back then. That was some forty-five years ago. In 1952." Mrs. Engstrom seemed pensive, lost in all those years. Then she said solemnly, "It grieves my heart, sometimes, when I think I might not see my boys in heaven. That's when I remember what Jesus said about not looking back."

Mrs. Engstrom's grief somehow spread to Annie's heart. The more she learned about the Bible and about heaven and hell, the more concerned she was about Stephen. What if she wouldn't see him in heaven? The very idea sent tingles of fear up Annie's spine.

"We'll keep praying for Stephen," Maggy said as if divining Annie's very thoughts.

"But my daughter, Martha. . .we called her Marty. . .knew the Lord before she died," Mrs. Engstrom said, continuing her story. "Poor Marty had cancer, you know. She suffered terribly. She died in 1987. Now I only have two daughters left— Dorean and Estelle." She smiled quite suddenly. "They're both retired. With good pensions, too. Dorean was a nurse, and Estelle was a schoolteacher like her mama." Mrs. Engstrom looked proud in a way only mothers were allowed. "But I remember when Estelle was twelve years old. I remember like it was only yesterday.

"Estelle had this idea that she was going to win the pie baking contest at the 4-H Club that year, but Marty was really the best baker in our household. Why, that girl could bake a lemon meringue pie that would set your mouth to watering for just looking at it!

"So, anyway, Estelle and Marty really got into a tiff over that contest, and you just won't believe what happened. It's quite a story! I just have to tell it. . ."

Annie and Maggy exchanged amused glances as if to say, "Here she goes again!"

❧

It was eight o'clock and just after the Sunday evening service when Dan offered to drop Mrs. Engstrom, Annie, and Josh off at their respective homes. It was dark already and the air held a bit of a bite. November was just around the corner. Soon it would be Thanksgiving. Then Christmas.

"I wish I knew where Stephen was," Annie said with a long sigh. Dan had just returned to the car from seeing Mrs. Engstrom safely into the retirement home. "I don't like to think of winter ahead and Stephen out in the cold."

"I know. But he may just come home once the weather starts really getting bad. That's when I wanted to go home. It's no fun being a runaway when you're cold and hungry."

Annie thought it over. "You know, sometimes I think jail would be the safest place for Stephen."

"Oh, I don't know about that," Dan replied. "I was involved in a prison ministry back when I was an undergrad, and jail for those guys was as tough as being on the streets."

"But what about one of those lock-in schools? At least if Stephen were in a facility like that, he'd be made to go to school and made to obey rules. I can't make him do anything!"

"Annie, God is better than jail. . .or a lock-in school."

"Yes, I suppose, but—"

Annie hesitated then, suddenly unwilling to share anymore. She was ashamed, really, of what she was feeling toward Stephen lately. A mother's love and concern, yes. However, there was fear, too, and a desire to see Stephen in a place where he was safe and where she didn't have to worry about him sneaking into the house, destroying and stealing things.

"What's up, Annie?" Dan said a little too perceptively.

"Oh, nothing," she replied.

Josh suddenly sprang forward, out of the backseat. "We don't want Stephen to come back home," he blurted. "Not if he acts crazy and steals from us to buy drugs. Right, Mom?"

Guilt assailed Annie. Coming from Josh, her feelings sounded callous and cold. Moreover, Annie noticed Dan's silence now. Was it a form of condemnation? Or was he just thinking?

"Dan, it's obvious that I can't manage Stephen," Annie said, hoping to explain herself. "And, to tell you the truth, I'm a little afraid of him right now. I mean, he turned my living room upside down, he's stolen things from me—things he knew were precious to me, and he said he hated me." Annie nearly choked on her last words.

"Annie, I can understand your feeling that way," Dan said, compassionately. "I really can understand. But God is more than able to protect you and Josh. . .and He can manage Stephen. Single-handedly and with His eyes closed!" Dan chuckled.

Annie even managed a smile at Dan's attempted humor.

He pulled the car up alongside the curb in front of Annie's house.

"Thanks for the ride, Mr. Brenshaw," Josh said. Then he opened the back door and climbed out of the car. "See ya at a quarter to eight tomorrow."

"Okay, buddy."

Josh ran for the house and Annie, too, thanked Dan. But as she went to get out of the front seat, he halted her with a hand on her arm. She looked at him expectantly, his features illuminated beneath the glow of the dome light. It was then that she realized Dan was struggling with what he wanted to say.

Finally he simply said, "Don't give up on Stephen, okay? I mean, I know it looks bad. . .maybe even hopeless. But as long as our God is on the throne, nothing is really impossible." He paused, wearing a somber expression. "I'm here as proof of that, Annie. What would I have done if my mother would have given up on me?"

Annie's heart instantly warmed to his cause as she recalled

her conversation with Mrs. Engstrom this afternoon. Then she remembered her decision to love Stephen regardless of his actions.

"Okay," she promised with a little smile. "I won't give up on Stephen."

"And don't be afraid of him. God does not give us a spirit of fear, but of power and of love and of a sound mind." Dan grinned. "Timothy 1:7."

Annie smiled. "I always ask for the reference."

"I know you do." His smile broadened. "The Bible also says that there is no fear in love; but perfect love casts out fear."

Annie was writing all this down on a piece of scrap paper she had in her purse.

"That's from 1 John 4:18."

"I'm going to look those passages up. I've got others from this afternoon, too."

"Good."

Annie tucked the paper and pen back into her purse and then looked back at Dan. "Thanks," she said. "I don't know what I'd do without you right now. Only a month ago, I felt like I had the weight of the whole world on my shoulders. But now I have some good friends in you and the Winstons. . .and God. I have a relationship with God, who is real and who cares about my kids and me!

"But, see, this is all new to me, Dan," she explained, "because all these years I've had to fend for myself." Annie opened the car door wider now and climbed out. "It's nice to know some reliable people who are willing to help me out right now.

"Well, see you later. And thanks again for the ride home."

"You're welcome," Dan said, smiling.

Annie closed the car door and gave a little wave. Then she turned and walked up the driveway to the side entrance of the house. Josh had gone in before her and had left the door wide open.

Walking into the kitchen, Annie closed the door and locked it. Then she resolved that everything would be all right. Everything would work out just fine. Even Josh's education at the

Academy. Somehow things would work out. *All I have to do,* she reminded herself, *is have faith as a grain of mustard seed. . .*

It was then that Annie realized she had somehow misplaced the packet of information that Mr. Wells had given her this morning. Had she left it at the Winstons? Annie didn't remember seeing it around. Where had it gone?

Finally she shrugged. *Oh well,* she thought, *I'll just have to get another information packet tomorrow.*

thirteen

Annie met with Mr. Wells, Deerwood Academy's principal, the following morning. She filled out and signed all the required forms; however, she was still concerned over how she would pay the tuition. To Annie, it was an exorbitant amount, but Mr. Wells kept saying that if it was indeed God's will, He would provide.

"And there are several church members who frequently sponsor children they feel have potential. Perhaps the Lord will lay the burden of Josh's tuition on someone's heart."

Annie nodded. She felt almost irresponsible—she was enrolling Josh in a private school she couldn't afford. Wasn't that irresponsible? Or was that trusting in the Lord?

"Don't worry, Mrs. Fetherston," the principal assured her. "We'll work with you regarding the tuition payments. The first one won't be due until the end of November."

Once more, Annie nodded. Then, after thanking Mr. Wells for his time, she left the school's office.

As the week progressed, Annie prayed frequently about the situation, asking the Lord to provide. She still believed God wanted Josh at the Academy. Each time she opened the Bible and read from the Word, she was convinced that Josh needed the structure, discipline, and encouragement the Christian school would give him. She was just nervous about how she was going to pay for it.

Meanwhile, Annie watched as her son came home looking "dead-dog tired," as Dan described it, from working at the Academy. Then, on Tuesday, the first day of November, Josh took placement tests that left him feeling especially exhausted. But the next morning he was up, dressed, and ready to go when Dan came by to get him. And there wasn't a single complaint about it, much to Annie's surprise.

❧

"Don't forget the lunches," she reminded Josh when he

almost left without them.

Annie had been preparing a lunch for Dan, too, when she made Josh's. . .just because Dan was so thoughtful to drive Josh to and from the Academy every day. Josh grabbed the two brown paper bags and ran out the front door.

"Did you make me one of those delicious lunches again today, Annie?" Dan called from the driveway, wearing a sheepish grin. "Bless your heart."

Annie smiled. "It's only PB and J today. Sorry. Nothing fancy."

"Aw, that's okay," Dan replied, feigning a disappointed shrug. "Except I think I'll have a bad day if you didn't pack some more of those homemade chocolate brownies."

Annie laughed. "Not to worry. The brownies got packed."

Dan smiled broadly while Josh bounded into the front seat of the car. Then Dan waved a good-bye to Annie before climbing back in behind the wheel. Moments later, he and Josh drove off together under the frosty November sky.

As she watched the car disappear down the street, Annie had a feeling that taking care of Dan Brenshaw might not be so terribly awful after all. It was obvious that he knew how to take care of himself. He always appeared to be well-groomed, and his clothes always looked clean. Dan's dress shirts, which he wore every day to school, looked crisp and wrinkle free. Moreover, he was an appreciative man, not an expectant one. And he had such a sensitive disposition. Very caring. Kind. . .

Stop it, Annie Fetherston, she told herself as she entered the kitchen and poured one more cup of coffee before she, too, had to leave the house. *Dan Brenshaw might be a handsome man, in a rugged sort of way, and he might have wonderful attributes. . .but he is not available. He's leaving in January. So quit your dreaming and get yourself ready for work!*

❧

Finally Saturday arrived, along with the bowling party, sponsored by Deerwood Bible Church's youth group, and even Annie was anticipating the fun. She thought she may have caught the enthusiasm from Josh; but, she had made some new friends herself. Jeff and Bonnie Randall, a brother and sister, were eager to have Annie join the singles group at church. They were going bowling tonight, too, and Annie thought that riding along with Jeff and Bonnie might take her mind off of Dan Brenshaw for a while. Why did that word "courtship" continue to roll around in her head?

If I make some more friends at church, Annie decided, then maybe it won't hurt so much when Dan leaves in January.

"Are you sure the bowling alley is big enough for both Deerwood Bible's youth group and the singles groups?" Annie teased when the Randalls came for her and Josh that evening. There were two more men in the car, sitting in the backseat. In fact, it was downright crowded in there!

Jeff was laughing at Annie's question. He was a short, stocky guy with an abundance of black, curly hair and Annie thought he looked about forty years old. However, he behaved like he could be part of the youth group—he had a fun-loving, laughing spirit that seemed rather contagious.

"Sure, there are plenty of lanes to go around," Jeff was telling her. "Are you a good bowler, Annie?"

"I don't know," she replied honestly as she climbed into the front seat of the Buick Century. It was Bonnie's car and Bonnie was driving. "It's been a long time since I went bowling."

"Well, I'll let you be on my team anyhow," Jeff said from the backseat. He moved over then, to make room for Josh.

Bonnie pulled away from the curb. "Jeff is very particular about who he lets on his bowling team, Annie," she said. "Consider yourself complimented."

Annie smiled. "Well, thanks, Jeff. I only hope you won't be disappointed."

"Me, too."

Everyone in the car chuckled at the remark.

They arrived at the bowling alley, checked in, and reserved their lanes. Most of the kids from the youth group had already arrived and were occupying the far right side of the alley—near the snacks and soda machines.

"Well, hello, Annie," Dan said, when they met by the racks of shoes. "I thought you weren't coming tonight. I guess you sort of gave me that impression. And then when the Winstons arrived and you weren't with them—"

"Josh and I came with the Randalls," Annie quickly

explained. "I met Bonnie last week, and she invited me to ride along with her and her brother, Jeff, tonight."

"I see." Dan was frowning a little and it caused Annie to wonder about it.

"Dan, Josh and I bother you enough for rides—"

"It's no bother, Annie. You know that."

Annie felt as though she was being reprimanded. Dan had asked her if she needed a ride tonight, but she had refused, having decided to come with the Randalls. It wasn't as if she and Dan had a commitment to each other. Dan, of all people, should know and understand that! He certainly was acting as if he didn't.

Not knowing what else to say, Annie selected a pair of bowling shoes, turned and walked back to where Jeff Randall was already throwing the first ball down the lane.

After two games Annie had had enough. She bowled a 74 and a 104—and that had been good, as far as she was concerned. Jeff, however, seemed disappointed with her scores. He even tried to give her a few pointers, standing behind her and showing her how to correctly hold the bowling ball before she rolled it toward the awaiting pins. But Jeff's instructions had only made Annie feel tense and foolish. . .and she sure hoped Dan Brenshaw wasn't watching. Jeff's arms had gone around her as he showed her how to hold the ball, and Annie could only imagine what that might have looked like to Dan. . . or anyone else watching. It had been both embarrassing and humiliating for Annie. She wished vehemently that she had not manipulated the circumstances tonight—she should have just come with Dan or the Winstons.

Selecting a seat on the brightly colored plastic spectator benches, near the center of the lanes, Annie sat down to watch for the rest of the evening. To her right, the youth group seemed to be having a fun time, and Annie chuckled watching some of the girls who continued to throw gutter balls. She suddenly wished she could say to Jeff Randall, "See, at least I'm not that bad!"

Dan appeared, surprising Annie, and handed her a can of cola. Then he sat down beside her.

"That's the Winstons' treat."

"Oh, that was nice. I'll be sure to thank them."

A moment of silence passed.

"Josh is a good bowler," Dan said on an easy note.

Annie smiled and sipped her drink.

"Doesn't take after his mom, I guess."

Annie nearly choked on the remark, feeling her cheeks flush with embarrassment. So, just as she feared, Dan had been watching.

For the next several moments they sat there as an uncomfortable silence grew between them. Annie didn't know what to say. Was she supposed to apologize? Except she hadn't done anything wrong!

Finally she said, "I guess Jeff and I are here tonight for two very different reasons. He came to win, and I came for the fun of it. I don't think Jeff appreciated my lack of. . .of seriousness for the game."

With a raised brow, Dan glanced her way. "Listen, Annie, I'm fairly well acquainted with Jeff and believe he's a sincere Christian man. However, he's here tonight to win more than just a bowling game." A little grin curved his mouth. "You, Annie Fetherston, have been set up."

"What?"

"You heard me."

She paused, looking at Dan in utter surprise.

"Jeff Randall got laid off from his job at the paper company, and he's been sharing an apartment with his sister, Bonnie, for the past couple of months. Driving her crazy, from what I hear—and I heard it from Jeff, himself! Anyway, he's looking for another job. But Bonnie's looking for a sister-in-law. Someone to take care of her brother. Someone to help him settle down. And you, Annie, are a prime target. You're a Christian, and you're a young, pretty widow. . ."

"All right, all right. I get the idea!" Annie's mind was screaming, Danger! Danger! Warning! Warning! All she had to hear were the words "take care of" and she was immediately alerted.

"I don't usually talk about folks, Annie," Dan continued, "but Maggy told me I should share that piece of information with you."

"Thank you," she replied a bit stiffly. Maggy knew about Annie's past relationship with Eric. . .except Annie wondered why Maggy didn't warn her herself. Why did it have to be Dan?

"It was bothering me, Annie," he said as if divining her thoughts. "It bothered me what I saw tonight and knowing the date was arranged without your knowledge. So when I announced to the Winstons that I was going over to talk with you, Maggy suggested I tell you about Jeff's circumstances as well as Bonnie's ulterior motive. It's really public knowledge. You're just too new to the church to know about it yet."

Annie felt like an idiot. She crossed her legs, encased in blue jeans, and twirled the can of cola between both hands.

"You're upset, aren't you? I can tell. When you get nervous or upset, you have a habit of playing with your drink, be it water or soda."

"I do?"

"Yes, you sure do."

Annie glanced over at Dan in surprise. She hadn't been aware that she had such a habit. "You must be very observant," she replied at last.

"Not usually." Then, before Annie could ask what he had meant by that, Dan said, "Don't feel too badly about this whole thing. I got it, too, when I first came to town. But I made a decision long ago to avoid the singles groups. They're not all bad. In fact, they're necessary. They're just not for me."

Annie nodded. "Me, either, I guess. I mean, I thought it was a good way to meet new friends. But I don't need that kind of. . .of pressure in my life."

Looking over at Dan again, she considered him. He was dressed casually in blue jeans and a baggy flannel shirt. Underneath that, he wore a long-sleeved, blue T-shirt that was visible only at the neckline and at his wrists where he had rolled up the sleeves of his flannel shirt. Annie thought he looked like a lumberjack and she couldn't help a little smile at the idea. Dan looked like he could be part of Rhinelander's logging museum. Maybe this town was affecting him more than he knew. Annie could only hope so. . .

Suddenly Dan caught her gaze and Annie looked away. She

found herself wishing then that she could share her feelings, yet she was afraid to verbalize them. Telling Dan that she was growing fonder of him with each passing day would make her feelings real somehow. But the end would only result in a real disaster when January came and Dan left Rhinelander.

"Well, you're not playing with your cola anymore," he said, "so you must be okay."

"Yes, I'm okay," Annie replied. "And thanks, Dan. I appreciate your concern. . .and your thoughtfulness."

He shrugged, looking a bit embarrassed.

"Can I be so bold as to ask for a ride home?"

Dan grinned. "Well, if you weren't going to ask, I was going to offer." He stood up. "I have to warn you, though, my car is going to be packed to the legal limit with teenagers."

Annie smiled. "I'll still take the ride. Thanks, Dan."

He nodded and turned to walk away but stopped after a few steps. Turning back, he indicated with another nod that she should follow him. It was an invitation, of sorts, to join in the fun with the youth group.

Annie smiled and got to her feet. The decision was a "no-brainer," as Josh would say. She definitely preferred being with Dan and the Winstons and a bunch of noisy teenagers than being set up. And later, Annie decided, she would politely let both Jeff and Bonnie Randall know it.

&

Late the following night, John Winston unknotted his tie. The day had been a long one, but it had been filled with many blessings, too. Annie and Josh had made public professions of faith this morning at church. Apparently Dan had spoken to them about it last night, and now the Fetherstons were in the process of joining the church. John was thrilled.

Maggy suddenly entered the bedroom. She had just come from settling baby Noah down for the night. He had been overly fussy, probably coming down with a little cold. But now all the kids were asleep. Taking off her robe and slippers, Maggy climbed into bed and snuggled beneath the covers.

"I'm glad you made a fire in the fireplace today," she said. "It was so cozy, so romantic."

John smiled. "That it was."

"It was a shame Mrs. Engstrom couldn't make it today, except it's understandable that she would rather spend some time with her daughters when she gets the chance."

John nodded absently as he readied himself for bed.

"And you didn't happen to notice Annie and Dan this afternoon, sitting side by side and talking, did you?" Maggy continued.

A slow grin formed on John's mouth. He knew what Maggy was insinuating. "Now, listen, I was in the living room the whole time and everything was right as rain. Josh was there, too."

Maggy gave him a look filled with innocence. "I was just asking if you noticed Dan and Annie. That's all."

John turned momentarily pensive. Dan and Annie did seem very friendly toward each other this afternoon.

"Yes, I noticed," he finally admitted.

"And?"

"And I hope that nobody gets hurt in all of this. Particularly Annie. I haven't heard that Dan changed his plans, and when he leaves, Annie is the one who's going to get left behind. It always hurts more, I think, to be the one left than the one doing the leaving."

Maggy pushed herself up on an elbow. "Oh, John, I never thought of it like that before."

"I know, honey."

"So now what?"

John shrugged. "We'll just have to keep praying and trusting that God is at work in this situation. The Lord knows that Dan fills a need in both our school and our church. Everyone likes him, and I know for a fact that Pastor Ashford has been encouraging Dan to stay. So maybe he will. On the other hand, if he ends up leaving, we can trust that God will fill the void. . .in our church and school, and in Annie's life, too."

fourteen

"Come on in, Annie," Charlene Hughes said, opening the front door of her home. "What's new?"

Annie smiled. It was going to take all afternoon to tell Char about all the new things in her life.

"What's your oldest kid up to? Is he behaving?"

Annie sighed. "Unfortunately, Char, I haven't a clue as to where Stephen is. He's been gone for over a month now."

"Oh, Annie, I'm sorry. Here, let me take your coat."

Shrugging out of her black wool winter coat, Annie handed it to Char, who hung it up in the front closet.

"I haven't given up on Stephen or anything," Annie added. "I keep praying for him."

Charlene nodded sympathetically.

"And speaking of praying. . .I've joined a church."

"Really? Which one?"

"Deerwood Bible Church. Josh started school at the Academy last week."

Charlene drew her chin back in surprise. "You won the state lottery and you didn't share it with me?"

Annie laughed. "Hardly. And I know you're probably wondering how I can afford a private school. The answer is. . .I can't. I'm just praying that God will provide somehow. I've started thinking that the 'somehow' might be in the form of me finding a second job." She shook her head. "Dan doesn't think so, though. He said getting a second job would be me providing for Josh's education, and Dan thinks I should let God provide."

"Let God provide? Like pennies from heaven?" Charlene laughed in a disbelieving way, but then suddenly she frowned. "Who's Dan?"

Annie had to smile. "How about we sit down and I'll tell you all about everything?"

"I just made a pot of flavored coffee. Let's sit in the kitchen where it's the warmest."

As they sat at the kitchen table, sipping the steaming, aromatic brew, Annie started relaying all that had taken place in the past weeks. It sounded incredible even to her own ears. Charlene was particularly curious about Dan Brenshaw.

"We're just friends, Char."

"A man and a woman cannot be 'just friends'."

"Well. . ." Annie paused, wondering if Charlene's last comment held some truth to it. The fact was, Annie had fallen in love with Dan and she had, at least, gotten to the point of admitting it to herself and to God. But what she should do about it next was still a mystery to her.

"My two-timing ex-husband can tell you all about the girlfriends he's had over the years."

Annie shook her head sadly. Charlene's ex-husband's unfaithfulness was still an open wound for her. The fact that they were women who had both lost their men, although in different ways, was the very foundation of Annie and Char's friendship. They had met years ago at the restaurant where Annie and Char once both worked as waitresses.

"So, do I get to meet this. . .this friend of yours?" Charlene asked in a tone laced with sarcasm.

Annie just shrugged. "Want to come to church with me next week? That would be the best time to meet him. Dan is the music director there, and he plays the piano. . .oh, Charlene!" Annie suddenly exclaimed. "You should hear this man play! He is so talented! But he's not conceited like you might expect someone so gifted to be. Dan is really very tenderhearted."

"Oh, really?"

Annie nodded. "And he's taken Josh under his wing, so to speak. Josh thinks the world of him. Dan has been helping me, too. He's been so supportive, especially concerning Stephen."

Char gave her a speculative glance. "Sounds like he's more than a friend, Annie."

"No. He's no more than a friend, Char, and I'm afraid that's all he'll ever be. You see, Dan is part of an evangelistic team. They travel around the country visiting one church after another, and right now Dan is just here in Rhinelander temporarily—to help out Deerwood Church and school with its music department." Annie got up from the kitchen table and set her empty coffee cup on the counter. "Dan is planning to leave in January."

"Well, maybe he'll change his mind," Charlene replied with a hopeful note.

Annie shrugged. She couldn't see that happening. Dan was very committed to his evangelistic team.

I'll just cry my heart out when he leaves, she thought, being facetious but utterly truthful with herself. *And Josh will probably cry right along with me.*

"Come on, Char," Annie said, purposely changing the subject, "let's get going on the housecleaning. I had better do a thorough job, too, since you're having guests on Thanksgiving Day."

Charlene rose from her chair. "Okay, okay, Annie. I can take a hint. I won't ask any more questions about this. . .this music man of yours."

"Good," Annie said, fishing out the furniture polish from the cabinet underneath Char's kitchen sink.

As it happened, Char agreed to attend the morning worship service with Annie the following Sunday. Annie knew, however, that it was curiosity alone that was bringing her. She even wondered if she ought to warn Dan. But then, on second thought, Annie realized it really wasn't necessary. She did tell Maggy—and Maggy, of course, was elated!

"And bring your friend to our Sunday afternoon dinner."

"Are you sure, Maggy?"

"Of course I'm sure."

Annie couldn't help but tease her then. "If you invite any more people to your Sunday afternoon dinner, Maggy, you and John are going to have to rent a hall!"

"Nonsense," Maggy retorted. Then she lifted a brow. "Don't tell me that, with all the time you're spending around Dan, his sense of humor is rubbing off on you. I won't be able to stand it!"

Annie felt her cheeks flame at the remark, and she tried to laugh it off. Then she went about her business even though Maggy's words continued to burn in her memory. *With all the time you're spending around Dan. . .*

Maybe I shouldn't be, she wondered. *But sometimes I don't even think I can help it!*

≫

It was the Sunday before Thanksgiving and the day was as bright as the sky was blue. Puffy, white cumulus clouds floated through the air, resembling clusters of cotton. The trees, however, were a stark contrast, bare and brown. They were a testimony to the fact that, though it was a beautiful day, winter was at hand.

Annie was particularly glad the worst winter weather was holding off because it meant that Stephen wasn't freezing to death somewhere, although northern Wisconsin had had its first frost weeks ago. Rhinelander had even seen a dusting or two of snow, but none of it stayed on the ground for more than a couple of days.

Charlene pulled up in her gold-colored Cadillac, an older model that she had purchased "dirt cheap" from someone she knew. Annie called for Josh, who came running down the stairs wearing a suit and tie. He had gotten a haircut after school one day last week—and all on his own, too. He even paid for it with the tip money he earned from his paper route. Josh had looked like a transformed young man before; but now, in a suit and tie, Annie scarcely recognized him.

"Where did you get those clothes?" she asked as her mouth dropped slightly in a pleasant surprise.

"They came in that box of stuff from Mrs. Miller," Josh replied. "Her boys are older than me, and they grew out of all these clothes. This suit was in the box. This dress shirt, too. Then the other day, Mr. Brenshaw showed me how to knot my tie. Did I do it okay?"

Annie smiled. "You did it just fine, Josh."

He beamed and then opened the front door. "Ladies first," he said, furthering Annie's surprise.

"Hey, maybe I should dress you up more often," she remarked, stepping outside.

Josh just shrugged, looking embarrassed as he pulled the front door closed behind him.

"Mr. Brenshaw wanted to know if we needed a ride today, but I told him we didn't because Char was picking us up. Then

Mr. Brenshaw asked me about fifty questions about her."

"About Char?"

Josh nodded as he reached the car. "Just basic stuff like how we know her."

"Oh." Annie paused before opening the front door on the passenger side.

"Mr. Brenshaw said I should call Char 'Mrs. Hughes.' He said that's more respectful since I'm a kid and she's a grown-up."

Annie smiled. "I appreciate that, Josh. . .your willingness to do what's right, I mean."

Josh nodded his reply and Annie pulled open the car door. "Hi, Char."

"Hi, Annie, get in. You, too, Josh."

"Yes, ma'am, Mrs. Hughes."

Annie almost giggled at Charlene's look of surprise. Josh was all dressed up and speaking so politely—he was a surprise to his mother, let alone a family friend who hadn't seen him since summertime.

"My goodness, Josh, you look like a million bucks!" Charlene exclaimed. "And you sound like such a refined gentleman." She looked at Annie. "I didn't know you were raising refined gentlemen."

Annie shrugged, wearing a helpless smile at the teasing. "What can I say, Char? Miracles do happen."

"I guess."

With that she pulled away from the curb and drove the six blocks to Deerwood Bible Church.

❧

Annie didn't have to wonder or fret over finding Dan so she could introduce Charlene; he found her shortly after the worship service.

"Josh told me you were bringing a friend," Dan said to Annie. Then he turned to Charlene. "Please to meet you. . . Mrs. Hughes, isn't it?"

"That's right." Char looked surprised and slightly overwhelmed. Annie had already introduced her to the Winstons, Lisa Johnson and her husband, the Millers, Bonnie Randall. . . and now Dan Brenshaw.

"Well, I'm pleased to make your acquaintance, ma'am," Dan drawled in a charming Texas accent that caused Annie to grin slightly.

Then he turned to Annie. "I'm not going over to the Winstons' place this afternoon. I felt obligated to accept another invitation."

Annie nodded in reply, but concealed her disappointment.

"I'll be there for Thanksgiving, though," Dan added, causing her to wonder if he'd been able to see right through her. Then his eyes sought hers earnestly. "You'll be there, too. . .right?"

"Right."

He nodded. "Well, that's good. I'm looking forward to it." He said it so tenderly, Annie felt as if he truly meant it. Such a simple statement, but it fueled a tiny, unbidden spark of hope in her heart.

Then Dan looked at Josh, standing right beside him. "Cowboys are playing the Packers on national TV Thanksgiving Day." Dan grinned. "And Dallas is gonna cream the Packers!"

"Not likely!" Josh retorted, grinning to match Dan's.

Annie smiled and rolled her eyes at Char, who was also smiling.

"Well, ladies—and Josh—I'll see you tonight."

"Bye, Dan."

He looked at Annie. "See you tonight."

"Oh, and it was nice to meet you," Char added.

"Likewise, ma'am." Then, with a grin for Josh, Dan turned and walked away.

"You know, that man could charm the birds right out of the trees," Charlene remarked as she and Annie strolled through the church's parking lot and toward the car. Josh had gone on ahead and now stood by the Cadillac, talking with another boy. "Of course," Char continued, "us northern women can be real suckers for blue eyes and a southern accent, can't we?"

"I suppose."

Annie laughed softly, wishing it were just that simple, and she marveled at how complicated feelings of love could be. And, here, poor Dan just thinks I'm a friend, she mused. He tried to warn me that he was leaving, but I guess my heart just wasn't paying attention.

Annie realized, then, that it was a good thing Dan wasn't going over to the Winstons' today. Perhaps, in this case, absence wouldn't make the heart grow fonder. Perhaps it would make the heart forget. Or at least come to its senses!

fifteen

Dan pushed the last of his peas around the plate and then set down his fork.

"Have you had enough to eat?" JoAnn Farley asked sweetly.

"Oh, I've had plenty. Thanks." Looking at Paul Farley, Dan added, "Your family is very fortunate to have such a good cook in a wife and mother."

"Yes, I know," replied Paul.

"Well, thank you," JoAnn replied, smiling at the compliment. She rose from the dining room table then and began to clear the dishes. Her two teenage daughters followed her into the kitchen, each carrying a plate.

Dan smiled over at Paul. "You have a fine family. Thank you for inviting me out today."

"Thanks for coming." Paul leaned forward with elbows on his wife's best, white-laced tablecloth. "What did you think of our girls' little piano recital?"

Dan grinned. "It was something all right. And to think they've never had a piano lesson in all their lives."

"They just make it up as they go along," Paul said, smiling proudly. "Isn't that amazing?"

"Amazing isn't the word for it, Paul." Dan replied, chuckling softly.

He had been subjected to nearly two hours of the Farley girls' piano playing, each pecking away at the keys with no rhythm or reason. They just. . .pretended to play. The piano, itself, needed a good tuning, and Dan had to force himself not to wince every time one of the girls struck a particularly bad key. But, all in all, it hadn't been so terrible.

"The fact that your girls can sit at the piano for such lengths of time," Dan added quite honestly, "makes me think they'd do well with lessons."

"What do they need lessons for?" Paul leaned back in his chair at the head of the table.

"Well," Dan began, "I guess it's a matter of discipline, really. Your daughters ought to learn how to read music, for instance, if they really want to play the piano in all seriousness. They should learn about sharps and flats and octaves. . .major and minor keys. . ."

Paul listened intently as Dan continued on his favorite subject.

Finally, they moved back into the living room where Paul opened his Bible. They talked about several passages and then shared their testimonies. Dan was impressed with how concerned Paul seemed in the area of soul-winning. Paul said both he and his wife frequently went out into their community and shared the gospel while they helped those in need, whether it be a meal or just companionship.

Suddenly JoAnn Farley appeared, carrying a tray with plates of sliced apple pie. Behind her, one of her daughters carried in the coffee.

"Time for dessert," she announced.

Then, as they ate, JoAnn pulled out a stack of papers. "I thought I'd share some of my writing with you," she said, looking at Dan. "I write poems and short stories. . .and I attend the School of the Arts here in Rhinelander every year."

"How nice," Dan remarked, noticing how quickly the Farley girls disappeared.

"Let me start with this story," JoAnn said. "I wrote it about a little blue jay I saw out my kitchen window last spring."

Paul yawned.

"Little blue bird in the budding tree," JoAnn began, "how I wonder what you're thinking. . ."

After JoAnn flipped over several pages, Dan ventured a look at his watch. He was amazed that someone could write so much about a bird's thoughts. Forcing himself to be attentive, Dan wondered where JoAnn was going with her story. Did it have a point? A few minutes later, Dan felt sure it didn't. It just meandered through the budding branches outside the Farleys' kitchen window. . .but maybe that's what it was supposed to do.

Dan had to smile, then, thinking that Annie would probably know what kind of story this was supposed to be. He thought Annie was an amazing woman—she read everything she could get her hands on. And, regarding the books that Dan shared with her, Annie always had intelligent responses that only seemed to increase his opinion of her.

"So, what did you think, Dan?" JoAnn asked, having finally finished reading.

"Hmmm. . ." Dan mulled it over. "Well, I'm no expert in literature, but I'd have to say that your piece was certainly. . . different."

"Oh, thank you!" she exclaimed happily. "I was trying to write something different."

Dan smiled a reply, glad to have said the right thing.

"I've got a talented family, don't I, Dan?"

"I should say you do, Paul." And, in his heart, Dan really meant that. These folks were kind and sweet spirited, not to mention generous with their hospitality.

"Well, I suppose I should get going," Dan said, rising out of the armchair.

JoAnn got his coat, and Paul walked him out the front door and to his car.

"Thanks for coming, Dan. It was important to my girls to play the piano for you—but I told you that when I invited you, didn't I?"

"Yes, you did."

"Well, I'm going to talk to them about piano lessons."

"Glad to hear it." Dan smiled and clasped hands with Paul. "And thanks, again. I enjoyed the fellowship today."

"We did, too."

Dan climbed into his car, started the engine, and then drove back to Deerwood Bible Church. He still had two hours before the evening service would begin, but Dan figured he could get some practice time in. Either that or paperwork.

Since the Farleys lived quite a way out of town, Dan had a good ten minutes of highway driving to do. He couldn't help but wonder, for about the third time this afternoon, what was happening at the Winstons'. Was Annie's friend a believer? Dan hoped that if she wasn't, she would be soon. No doubt Mrs. Hughes could see the changes in Annie and Josh and those changes alone would be powerful testimonies of Jesus Christ in their lives.

Dan smiled. It thrilled him to watch the Fetherstons grow, and he was glad that they were now part of a good Bible-preaching church. He felt confident that Annie and Josh would be fed spiritual "meat" and would be able to continue to grow in the Lord.

Then Dan paused to reflect on the way most folks at Deerwood faithfully witnessed for the Savior. He thought it was admirable that they were concerned about their community and committed to reaching out and involving themselves in it. In fact, Dan occasionally wished that Deerwood Bible Church was his church home.

"Except that's impossible!" he declared out loud. "I'm leaving in January, and my mind's made up. I've got a heart for evangelism—"

Dan cut himself short, realizing, then, that he had just been thinking about how the people of Deerwood Bible Church shared his burden for reaching the lost—he could have a heart for evangelism right here.

"Nope, I'm leaving!" he declared once more, yet he somehow knew that he was fighting a losing battle. It was a heart-versus-the-head battle, and since Dan was aware of his weaknesses and understood that he was quite headstrong, he thought this could prove to be a fight to the death. The death of what, however, was still to be determined. Would it be his ministry? Not likely. Dan was confident that he could continue his music ministry here. What about the death of his bachelorhood? Now there was a real concern!

Dan immediately thought of Annie Fetherston. If there was ever a woman he would be inclined to pursue romantically, it'd be Annie. He thought she was pretty. . .and she possessed a hunger for the things of God. She had a sweet spirit that somehow tugged on Dan's heartstrings, and though she wasn't formally educated, Annie was intelligent. She had a desire to learn, and Dan had a desire to teach her—a fact that made Dan uncomfortable to even admit. But it was there. Dan had special feelings for Annie. It was true. And Dan had to confess to being downright jealous when he saw her bowling with Jeff Randall!

Pulling into the church's lot, then, Dan parked his car and

shut off the engine. *Lord,* he breathed in prayer, *I know I'm called to full-time service, and I'm committed to my evangelistic team, but I sure didn't count on meeting Annie when I accepted this six-month term here in Rhinelander. So now what do I do? Lord, I need Your help.*

The evening service was about to begin, and Dan sat down at the piano. He began to play some background music while people got settled, and he decided to play Annie's song. . . that's what he had come to think of it as: "Annie's Song." It was the one he had her listen to in the restaurant—the song he was in the process of composing.

Dan couldn't help a glance in her direction. She was sitting with the Winstons and Mrs. Hughes, who had come back again this evening. Dan had heard that Mrs. Hughes didn't know the Lord and, apparently, she really didn't care to at this point. Dan thought that the fact Mrs. Hughes came back tonight was a victory in and of itself.

And then, as if Annie suddenly recognized the piece he was playing as hers, she turned to look at him. Their eyes met, and a knowing smile passed between them. It gave Dan a special feeling inside, too. It was like a shared secret between two good friends.

And I'm crazy, Dan decided, looking back down at the piano keys. *I'm crazy to think I'm going to walk away from this church and that woman unscathed!*

❧

Thanksgiving Day arrived and the weather was extraordinary for one of the last days in November. Rhinelander had been experiencing an unseasonably warm spell. . .if fifty-five degrees could be considered warm. Dan was sure that winter had come, but longtime residents in that small, northern Wisconsin town knew better. Subzero temperatures lurked around the corner.

Regardless, the weather was beautiful today, and Annie had made up her mind to enjoy it. She didn't want to worry about Stephen, today. . .or money, or unpaid tuition. Annie just wanted to give thanks to God for her blessings, among them being her job, a roof over her head, food to eat, and plenty of new friends who cared about her.

Josh, on the other hand, was just excited about watching the Packers play the Dallas Cowboys on national television today. Dan and John Winston seemed as excited. John had invited another teenager, a young man by the name of Billy Smith. Billy was a new Christian, too, and his parents were divorced. He only saw his father alternate weekends, and since his mother had to work today, John asked Billy to be part of their Thanksgiving Day celebration. The young man was thrilled to be asked, and with his mother's approval, he accepted the invitation.

"Are you ready, Mom?" Josh called from the living room. "Mr. Brenshaw just pulled into the driveway."

Annie had just pulled the cheesy potato casserole from the oven. She had baked two pumpkin pies and made one of the main dishes in order to help Maggy out with the cooking.

"Tell Mr. Brenshaw that I'll be right out," she replied. "I just need to wrap this up."

"Okay."

With oven mitts protecting her hands, Annie covered the glass baking dish with aluminum foil. Then she placed it in a cardboard box, insulated on the bottom with another pair of oven mitts.

"Need some help?" Dan asked, coming through the side door moments later. Josh was right behind him, following like a shadow.

"As a matter of fact," Annie replied, smiling a greeting at Dan, "could you carry this box for me? But be careful, it's hot."

"Smells great."

Annie's smile broadened.

"My mom makes it every year," Josh said. "It's got grated cheese and potatoes and milk and butter."

"Sounds almost as good as it smells," Dan replied. Then he turned to Josh and tossed the car keys to him. "Open the trunk for me, will you, buddy?"

"Sure."

Josh ran outside ahead of Dan who followed, carrying the box of bubbling hot potatoes. Then Annie pulled on her coat, swung her purse over her shoulder, and picked up the box that contained the two pies. Minutes later, the food packed and the passengers secured, Dan backed the car out of the driveway and drove the distance to John and Maggy Winstons' place.

The plan was that dinner would be served before the Packers/Cowboys game. Maggy remarked that she disliked planning her Thanksgiving Day meal around football. However, she maintained a sweet spirit about it that impressed Annie. They worked side-by-side in the kitchen while Mrs. Engstrom chattered away amicably. She was especially pleased today because her daughters had been invited, too, and were expected to arrive shortly.

"Dan and I are going out for a case of pop and a bag of ice," John announced, coming into the kitchen. "Between the nice weather and throwing the football around outside, I think we might run out. We'll be back soon."

Maggy nodded. "Okay."

"Josh and Billy are still passing the ball outside in the front yard and the girls are on the porch with the baby."

With a smile, Maggy replied, "I'll keep an eye out for them."

John chuckled at the cliché and then he and Dan left for the store.

"That's one nice thing about owning a grocery store," Maggy said to Annie and Mrs. Engstrom. "Even though we're closed to the public, John has the key so we're set if a need arises."

The comment sent Mrs. Engstrom off on a tangent about the year Aunt Eleanor cooked the turkey until it was dry as old bones and Uncle Frank had to fetch another at the last minute.

⁊⁊

Dan waited in the mini-van while John ran into Paradigm Foods. He emerged no more than five minutes later with a bag of ice cubes and two 8-packs of soda.

"I've got Pepsi products on sale this week," John said, opening the side of the van and depositing the items. "I grabbed one 8-pack of Mountain Dew and another of Diet Pepsi. . .for those on a diet today."

Dan chuckled. "Won't be me."

"Me neither," John said as he climbed into the van. "Hey, you mind if I stop for gas on the way home?"

"No, go ahead."

John drove to a small gas station and pulled up to the pumps. He hopped out of the van, but this time Dan got out, too. Walking around the vehicle, Dan leaned against the back quarter panel so he and John could talk while the pump was running.

Then suddenly John got a funny look on his face. "Don't turn around too quickly," he said, "but I think that's Annie's son Stephen over there. . .behind the station with that bunch of kids. I've only seen him once—when he came into Paradigm Foods with Josh. It was last summer. . .but I think that's him, the kid with the dark hair. . .wearing the ponytail."

Slowly, Dan turned around and spotted the young man whom John had just described. "You really think it's him?"

"Reasonably sure. But, as I said, I've only seen him once before."

Dan considered the group. There were five young men standing around an old Plymouth Duster. Heavy metal rock and roll blared from the car stereo, and Dan was instantly reminded of the horrible pit and miry clay from which he was delivered.

"Let's go talk to them."

"Are you out of your mind?"

"No." Dan grinned. "Not any more than usual."

John grew serious and considered the idea. "We would be taking a chance, Dan. These kids may be into drugs and may even be armed and dangerous."

"I think it's a chance worth taking."

John shrugged. "Okay. Head on over. I'll finish up here, pay for my gas, and then meet you."

Dan nodded. Then, sending up a quick prayer for wisdom, he walked first in the direction of the station, taking the sidewalk around to the back. He thought that even the slightest element of surprise would be to his advantage. Coming up on the kids, however, it was Dan who was surprised since it took a good long moment for any of them to realize he was there. The music, screaming out of the car stereo, was just that loud!

When they finally noticed him, one of the boys turned it down.

"What's up, mister?" asked a boy with pink hair. He gazed at Dan warily. "You a cop?"

The boys seemed restless, ready to run, until Dan shook his

head. "I'm a musician, and I. . .well, I happened to notice that you all are music lovers. I could hear your music clear across the station lot."

"Good stuff, ain't it?" asked one of the others. "Name of the group is Bondage."

Dan smiled slowly. He thought he recognized bondage when he heard it. Then he chuckled inwardly—his definition was quite different from that of the boy's. However, Dan knew right where these kids were coming from. He'd been there once himself.

Dan turned toward the young man with the ponytail then. He was tall, broad-shouldered, and clad in denim, except for a plain white T-shirt that he wore under his jacket. "You wouldn't happen to be Stephen Fetherston, would you?"

The boy took a deep draw off the cigarette he held, but his chocolate brown eyes widened at the question. "What's it to ya?" he shot back.

"Well, I'm a friend of your mom's. . .and I know Josh."

A few jeers emanated from the group. "It's Mommy's friend, Stevie," someone teased in falsetto.

Dan just kept his gaze on Stephen who, in spite of his friends, kept looking back at Dan. Then he narrowed his eyes suspiciously. "A friend of my mom's?" It seemed he didn't believe it.

"I know your mom and Josh through the Winstons," Dan explained. "The Winstons own Paradigm Foods. . .where your mom works. And this is where I work," he added, handing Stephen a tract. He pointed to the backside where the address and phone number of Deerwood Bible Church were printed.

Stephen didn't even look at it before shoving it in his jacket pocket.

"Well, I hope you boys have a good Thanksgiving Day," Dan said, sensing that he had made as much progress as possible. . .for now. "Oh, and, Stephen," he couldn't help but add, "your mom, Josh, and I will be at the Winstons' today. Your mom made the best-looking cheese-and-potato dish I ever saw. I can't wait to dig into it. We're going to have turkey and stuffing and sweet potatoes. . .oh, yeah, and your mom's home-made pumpkin pies. Man, did those pies smell delicious!"

Dan had to force himself not to laugh for suddenly he had won the attention of all five boys. Dan could practically hear their mouths watering.

"Who cares," Stephen finally replied, but Dan didn't think he meant a word of it. On the contrary, Dan sensed that Stephen cared enough to look absolutely miserable.

"You can always go home, Stephen," he said just above a whisper. "Even this afternoon, you could choose to come over to the Winstons' place, fill your belly, and reconcile with your mom."

As if in reply, Stephen threw his cigarette at Dan's booted feet. Dan met the young man's rebellious, dark gaze with one of deep concern. Then, slowly, he ground out the cigarette with his heel.

"I've got a feeling that you and I will meet again sometime, Stephen," he drawled in a friendly warning.

With that, Dan turned and walked away, catching up to John just as he came out of the gas station.

sixteen

Annie leaned her forearms over the wrought iron front porch railing. Between her hands she held a can of diet soda, twirling it around.

"You're upset, aren't you?" Dan remarked, standing beside her.

Annie stopped twirling the soda can. "Oops, sorry."

Dan laughed. "Don't be sorry. . .but don't be upset, either. I was really encouraged this afternoon. I got to meet Stephen."

Annie sighed. "But he was smoking a cigarette. I was so stupid to believe him when he told me he didn't smoke. Maybe it's really true about the drugs. . .and God only knows what else."

Dan nodded. "And that's the key right there, Annie. God knows. Even when we don't understand. He does."

"But what am I going do about Stephen?"

"What can you do, Annie? Watch and pray. I think that's about all at this point." Dan paused. "But I'm telling you, I recognized something in his eyes this afternoon. He's not happy, and that's good. Maybe it'll be what brings him home."

"And then what do I do with him?" Annie exclaimed.

"Remember the story of the Prodigal Son?"

Annie nodded, though grudgingly.

"You're just going to have to love the kid right through this. The Bible says that love is strong as death. Now that's mighty powerful, wouldn't you say?"

Annie looked over at him. "Where—?"

"Song of Solomon." Dan grinned. "I knew you were going to ask. It's the last chapter, and I know that for a fact because it was part of my devotional reading the other day." Dan shook his head and his grin faded. "Song of Solomon is not the book I would choose to be reading right now. . .but I guess it's what the Lord wants me to read, 'cause there it was right in front of my face!"

127

Annie frowned, feeling puzzled. "What are you talking about?"

"Oh, I can't say, Annie," Dan said apologetically. "But I can tell you this: the Lord is working me over something fierce!"

"Sorry to hear that," Annie replied, unsure of what else to say.

Dan only laughed. "There you go, being sorry again. Don't be," he said gently. "This is the refining fire of God—it's just that my flesh is screaming."

"I suppose."

Annie was still puzzled as to what Dan was experiencing. But she had heard Maggy talk about the Spirit and the flesh during a Bible study one Sunday. Maggy said they waged war against each other because the flesh was a person's sinful nature and the Spirit was God's Holy Spirit.

"You know, I believe Stephen has your eyes, Annie," Dan said as he looked right into them.

Annie held his gaze, feeling that unwanted spark growing a little stronger in her heart.

"You've got beautiful eyes."

She smiled demurely. "Thanks, Dan."

Then Annie looked the other way in an effort to conceal her emotions. She felt both flattered and bewildered by Dan's comments about her "beautiful eyes." Didn't he know such sayings affected a woman's heartbeat in the most amazing way?

He thinks we're just friends, Annie thought. *Maybe I ought to tell him that I feel more for him than I would a casual friend.*

"I suppose the rest of Stephen resembles his dad, though," Dan continued in a lazy-sounding drawl. "Am I right? Does he favor his father?"

Annie looked back at Dan, her bearings regained, and nodded. "I always thought Stephen looked more like Eric, whereas Josh is somewhat of a mix between the two of us." She smiled.

Dan seemed thoughtful for several long moments. "So what was he like, anyway? Eric, I mean."

Annie was momentarily nonplussed by the question. She didn't really mind sharing things about her deceased husband with Dan, and yet she was utterly baffled at the fact he was asking. And during the Packers/Cowboys game at that—and Dallas was winning!

"Am I getting too personal again, Annie?" Dan asked, looking sheepish. "It's that hoof-in-mouth thing, I guess."

Annie laughed. "Oh, it's all right. I don't mind telling you about Eric except there's not a whole lot to tell. And I suppose you're just wondering because of your friendship with Josh."

Dan gave a little shrug.

"Well, Stephen probably remembers more about his dad than Josh does anyway. Eric was a truck driver and a very busy man. He had a lot of friends and an equal amount of hobbies, so his lifestyle was not conducive to building family relations."

"You say that so flippantly, Annie," Dan remarked. "Doesn't it hurt?"

"Not anymore," she replied in all honesty. "While the boys were still babies I realized that I wasn't going to change Eric, and I was tired of trying, so I just gave up. I did what I had to do, and he did what he wanted to do. That's how it was.

"But don't get the wrong idea, Dan," Annie quickly added. "Eric always made sure the bills were paid, and I always had grocery money. And he made sure the kids and I had the things we needed."

"Except he withheld the most important thing," Dan said. "Himself."

Annie shrugged.

"I mean, look at the Winstons, for example. I know John works at spending quality time with his kids and Maggy."

"Yes, but most marriages aren't like the Winstons' marriage." Annie paused before confessing, "I wondered for a long time if the two of them just put on a good show or if they were for real."

"They're for real."

Annie nodded. "I know that now. The Winstons are one of those storybook couples."

"How about one of those Christian couples, Annie?" Dan said suggestively. "When two people love the Lord first, with all their hearts, souls, and minds, it inevitably shows in their love for each other." Dan paused reflectively. "I remember when Mike Pettit did a series on marriage. He incorporated 1 Corinthians, Chapter 13 into 1 Peter, Chapter 3. Then he concluded with the last part of Ephesians, Chapter 5." He paused once more. "Maybe you should do a personal study on those passages of Scripture, Annie."

A wave of longing, combined with intense confusion, flooded her senses. Annie wished she could be honest with Dan, and she wished Dan would love her right back. But neither seemed possible. Was Dan so unaware of her as a woman that he could speak candidly of love and marriage and not expect her to react?

Feeling suddenly irritated, Annie turned and looked him square in the eyes. "Why should I do that, Dan?" she asked on a challenging note. "Why should I study those passages?"

Dan narrowed his gaze as if attempting to see right through her and into her heart and soul, but Annie wasn't about to let that happen. Yes, he might be the man who had stirred up feelings she never thought she'd feel again, but he was also leaving in little better than a month. Annie's heart was already breaking.

"I was just trying to help, Annie," Dan said at last.

"I know. And you've been a big help. I appreciate everything you've done for Josh and me." Annie began twirling her soda can again. "But I think you're getting in way over your head. You're getting in too deep, Dan."

He pursed his lips in momentary thought. "I guess it's my choosing."

Annie shook her head. "Not when you're going to pull others in with you. They might not be as strong as you are."

"Meaning?"

Annie shook her head. She disliked the hyperbole, and yet she wasn't brave enough to speak her mind directly. Squaring her shoulders, she finally replied, "You know, I wonder how the Packers are doing."

"Annie—" Dan's tone held a subtle warning.

"I don't know about you, but I'm going to find out the score."

"Hold on a minute."

Annie refused and strode quickly to the house. She opened the front door and headed for the kitchen where Maggy was just slicing one of the pumpkin pies.

"Want to have dessert with us, Annie?" she asked. "We ladies are ignoring the men and the football game altogether."

"That's right," said one of Mrs. Engstrom's daughters. "And we're having a fine time of fellowship while we're doing it, too."

Annie smiled. "I believe that's just what I need," she replied, accepting a piece of pie from Maggy. Ignoring the men sounded like the best idea she'd heard in a long time. And there was one man in particular she'd like to ignore, too. Dan Brenshaw!

❧

"I don't know, Dan, I guess I thought you'd be more excited about the Cowboys beating the Packers today."

Dan glanced over at John and forced a smiled. "Oh, I've just got a lot on my mind right now. Don't take it personally."

"Okay, I won't." John was momentarily thoughtful. "Anything you want to talk about?"

"Not right now. I've just got a lot of decisions to make."

"Hmm. . .and you don't want to pass the football out front with Josh and Billy?"

"Not just now."

"Okay."

The two men sat in the family room, watching the post-game program. Dan couldn't even say what was happening on the TV, he was so engrossed in his thoughts. All he knew was that Annie made some of the most curious comments outside on the front porch, and now he was trying to figure out what it all meant.

She said I'm in too deep. . .but too deep in what? Dan wondered. *Josh's life? Was that it? Or was she talking about herself?*

Dan finally decided that he had just gotten too personal. He had hit a nerve by asking Annie about her marriage—and it sounded like she wasn't interested in getting married again, either. Maybe that's what she meant by "in too deep."

She thinks she's going to break my heart, Dan thought,

trying not to grin. *Well, that's real sweet of her. . .but that's Annie. Real sweet. And maybe even a real challenge.* Dan shook his head. *Lord, You know I can't resist a challenge.*

Immediately that old sinking feeling set in, and Dan realized once more the enormity of the decisions he faced.

And then it hit him. Maybe, this really isn't such a big deal after all. Maybe I'm the one making it a big deal because I'm not trusting the Lord like I should.

"You sure you don't want to talk about it, Dan?" John asked once more. He had a concerned expression on his face. "I mean, you seem. . .oh, I don't know. . .troubled."

"Naw," Dan drawled with a genuine smile now. "I'm all right. . .and I've just got to trust the Lord to lead me through this." He paused and tried to give John a reassuring nod. "I realized, just moments ago, that I've been trying to do much too much in my own strength instead of depending on God. Coming to that realization, I believe, was half of what I've been battling."

John smiled. "It's good you came to that understanding, Dan, but it's an easy battle to lose. I struggle with it daily."

Dan nodded, and he felt more peace in his heart at that moment than he'd had in a whole month.

"Yeah, okay, let's go pass the football," Dan said, standing up. "I think I better work off those two pieces of pumpkin pie I ate. . .not to mention everything else."

John rose from the recliner and laughed. "You're on, Mr. Dallas Cowboys fan."

❧

It was nearing eight o'clock when Annie finally rounded up Josh and her baking dishes. Dan was going to drop them off after he drove Billy home. One of Mrs. Engstrom's daughters had already left with her sister and mother. This Thanksgiving Day celebration had come to its close.

Annie's disposition had changed dramatically during the course of the afternoon. Something Mrs. Engstrom said affected her deeply with regards to her feelings for Dan. Mrs. Engstrom had said, "My advice to young people is—enjoy whatever blessings God sends your way to the fullest! They might be here today and gone tomorrow, you never know. So enjoy them while you can."

"And what do you advise when a. . .a blessing is taken away?" Annie couldn't help asking, thinking of Dan's plans to leave in January.

The question, however, didn't stump Mrs. Engstrom in the least. "In the words of Job, dear, 'The Lord gave, and the Lord hath taken away; blessed be the name of the Lord.' And that should be our response, too."

Annie had been immediately humbled. She realized, then, how selfish she was behaving, expecting Dan to stay for her purposes when it was the Lord and His work that came first! But she could cherish Dan's company now and enjoy his music while he was here.

As Dan pulled up to the curb in front of their house, Annie handed the keys to Josh and asked him to unlock the front door.

"I just want to have a couple words with Mr. Brenshaw before I come in."

"Okay, Mom," Josh replied. "Are we still playing football tomorrow afternoon?" he asked Dan.

"You bet. I'll come and pick you up, and then we'll go get Billy."

Josh nodded, closing the car door.

Dan turned to Annie. "How 'bout I walk you up the driveway while we talk."

Annie nodded and climbed out of the car.

"Listen," she said as they met on the sidewalk, "I'm sorry about this afternoon. . .when we were talking on the front porch."

Dan chuckled softly. "What are you sorry about?"

Annie shrugged. "Dodging your last question, I guess."

"That's okay. I shouldn't have gotten so personal."

Annie paused to collect her thoughts and emotions. Finally, she said, "I'm thankful that God brought you to Rhinelander, Dan. And, when January comes and you leave to join your evangelistic team, I'm going to still be thankful."

Dan pursed his lips in momentary thought and then laughed. "You'll be thankful to see me go, huh? Have I been that much of a pest, Annie?"

The tension between them was immediately lifted, and

Annie laughed, too. "You know what I mean, Dan."

"Of course I do. . ."

"Mom!" Josh cried, bursting out of the side door. "Stephen's here. And he's got his jerky friends with him!"

Annie's legs suddenly felt as though they were made of gelatin, and as if sensing it, Dan grabbed hold of her elbow.

"I'll walk you inside, Annie," he said, sounding calm and collected.

Gratefully, she nodded.

Josh ran in ahead of them, and by the time Annie and Dan reached the living room, a verbal exchange was taking place between the two brothers.

"There'd be something to watch if you hadn't stolen our TV!" Josh exclaimed.

"Buzz off, punk," Stephen replied, inhaling deeply on his cigarette.

His friends laughed.

Annie was suddenly outraged at Stephen's boldness. How did he ever come to think he could smoke openly in her house?

"Put out that cigarette, Stephen," she said in her sternest voice. "You know smoke bothers me."

"Dad used to smoke," he replied arrogantly. "But you didn't let him smoke in the house either, did you?"

Annie had to force herself not to react indignantly. "Your dad wasn't a regular smoker," she finally managed. "He only smoked with his friends. . .when they went out together. Now put out that cigarette!"

Much to Annie's astonishment and relief, Stephen complied. He extinguished the cigarette by dropping it in a soda can.

"This your new boyfriend, Mom?" Stephen asked in that same tone of arrogance, except now he was looking directly at Dan.

"Dan is a friend, if that's what you mean, yes."

"Oh, yeah, that's what he said this afternoon. He's a friend."

"You got a problem with that, Stephen?" Dan asked in a tone that beheld a slight challenge.

"Yeah, he's got a problem with it!" one of the boys replied, getting up off the couch. Annie recognized him at once as Pink Top Pete and she sensed real trouble here.

"Josh," she said, not even daring to take her eyes off the other boys, "call the police."

Josh fairly ran into the kitchen, and Annie heard him pick up the telephone.

"Leave my mom alone," Stephen said, standing up now, too. The other boy, Ed, stood as well. A trio of trouble, all glaring at Dan.

"You want me to leave you alone, Annie?" Dan asked with a slightly amused grin on his face.

"No, I don't," Annie replied quickly. She gave her son a hard look. "Stephen, Dan has been a big help to me."

Stephen's face reddened with irritation. "He's the one who gave you that. . .that Bible, isn't he? And that's when you changed. . .everything in this house changed! I couldn't even live here anymore!"

Annie nervously chewed her lower lip.

"The police are on their way, Mom," Josh said, coming from the kitchen.

"Let's roll, man," Pete said, leading the boys toward the front door.

Stephen was the last to follow, and he paused in front of Annie. "I want you to stay away from this guy. . .that is, if you ever want me to come home again."

"Oh, Stephen, no, don't give me an ultimatum. You should be happy for me. You said I didn't have any friends and all I did was work, work, work. But now I've got some very nice friends. . .and Dan is one of them."

"But I didn't mean for you to go out and try to replace Dad!"

"I'm not trying to replace your dad," Annie gently stated.

"Then change back to the way you were. . .before you started going to church and before Josh started going to that preppie school. And get this guy out of our house! He can't take Dad's place. . .not ever!"

"Shut up, Stephen!" Josh hollered from his place beside Dan. "You don't even know what you're talking about. Mr. Brenshaw is—"

Dan was shaking his head slightly at Josh in an effort to forestall further comment. Josh took the hint and quieted.

"See what I mean?" Stephen shouted. "He thinks he can take Dad's place with Josh!"

"That's not true, Stephen. Dan is just a friend. He's Josh's friend, too."

"I'd like to be your friend as well, Stephen," Dan said on a note of genuine sincerity. "Will you give me a chance?"

Before Stephen could answer, Ed was at the door. "C'mon, man, the cops'll be here any minute! We gotta run for it, or we'll never make it back to the car!"

Stephen hesitated momentarily, but then flew out the door and ran like the wind down the sidewalk behind his friends. Watching from the front door, Annie didn't know whether to be relieved or worried—so she decided on a little bit of both.

Then she turned to Dan who was smiling from ear to ear. "What's so funny?" she asked helplessly.

"Annie," he said, "I think we've finally got that boy's attention!"

seventeen

The following afternoon was another football game with several of the teenage boys from the youth group. The day was cloudy and cold, but in spite of the weather, kids from the neighborhood began to show up at the field and were invited to play, too. Many parents had to go back to work today, being the day after Thanksgiving and a busy shopping time; however, two fathers arrived in time to help Dan referee the game.

Throughout the afternoon, Dan spotted that old Plymouth Duster in which Stephen Fetherston and his friends were most likely living. Dan guessed as much from all the junk he had seen in the backseat of the car, though he hadn't mentioned that to Annie. Why upset her further? Dan wished the boys would join the game today. Nothing like a good football game to get to know what somebody else is really made of. At least that's the way Dan saw it. But Stephen and his friends didn't seem interested in playing, just staking out the game from the car.

It began to get dark around 4:30 P.M. and everyone packed up their gear and left the football field. Dan drove Billy home and then pulled into Annie's driveway and left Josh off.

"Tell your mom hello for me."

"Okay," Josh replied. Then he seemed to grow momentarily pensive. "Mr. Brenshaw?" he asked. "Was Stephen right yesterday. . .I mean, even just a little right?"

"In what way, buddy?"

"About you. . .and my mom."

Dan didn't know how to answer that exactly. He knew kids could be extremely perceptive, whereas adults tended to ignore or hide their feelings. Dan often wondered what happened between those years of transparent innocence and guarded mistrust. And Dan couldn't say he wasn't guilty of the latter, either.

"Josh," he finally replied, "I like your mom a whole lot. I
137

really mean that. It's just that I'm supposed to leave in January and I don't want her feelings to get hurt. Know what I mean?"

Josh nodded. "Except they're already gonna get hurt. Me and my mom have already decided that." He shrugged. "My mom said that happens sometimes."

"I suppose it does." Dan imagined that his feelings were going to get a little hurt in all this, too.

"Of course," Josh said, sounding very diplomatic, "you could always change your mind and stay here and marry my mom. That'd be awesome! Or maybe you could take me and my mom with you!"

Dan was grinning broadly. He had thought those very same thoughts at least five times in the last two days. "Well, Josh," he said at last, "I'll remember what you suggested. Okay? But that's all I can promise at this point."

Josh nodded. "Okay. See ya, Mr. Brenshaw. I gotta hurry up and do my paper route now."

Dan nodded. "See ya, Josh."

With that, he backed out of the driveway, then drove down the street. At the corner, he passed the Duster, parked on the other side. Feeling like a smart alec, Dan waved to the boys as though they were all friendly neighbors in passing. Then he chuckled to himself. But his amusement faded as the Duster followed him. . .all the way back to his small, furnished apartment that the church rented for him. It was situated above a sewing supply store on the edge of town.

Dan parked his car and then climbed out. He walked over to the kids in the Duster, and the boy with the pink hair rolled down the window. Dan nearly had to take a step back when the heavy smell of cigarette smoke hit him.

He managed a grin anyway. "You boys want to come up for a while? Is that why you followed me home?" Dan knew that wasn't the case, but he wasn't going to let three teenage kids get the best of him. "I've got some leftover turkey. We can make sandwiches. Then I'll show you from the Bible how you can be saved and on your way to heaven. What do you say?"

"I say forget it!" said Stephen from the backseat, piled high with junk. "And we followed you because I wanted to know where you live."

He spoke the words like a threat, but Dan refused to be intimidated.

"Well, now you know, so visit any time you like."

Dan turned and walked away, but the hairs on the back of his neck prickled. Dan knew those boys were of a mind to do more harm than good. However, he also knew that if they sensed even the slightest bit of fear in him, he'd never win them over.

Opening the door to his apartment, Dan recited a portion of Psalm 91. "For he shall give his angels charge over thee, to keep thee in all thy ways. They shall bear thee up in their hands, lest thou dash thy foot against a stone." Dan paused in the hallway, closing the heavy glass-panel door behind him. "Or lest thou run into three mighty tough teenage boys," he added, looking back at the car.

Turning from the door, Dan knew he could do nothing else but leave this situation in God's hands. Then, on newly determined strides, he made his way up the stairs to his apartment.

❧

As the days passed, Dan watched for the Plymouth Duster and saw it almost everywhere he went. One night the boys even parked right beside his car, and Dan, having worked late, was forced to walk out into the dark parking lot, praying that he wasn't going to have a fight on his hands. Or worse. But the kids didn't do anything. They didn't even shout threats at him or throw their cigarette butts out the window at him, both of which had occurred in times before. No, this time, they just sat there while Dan started his car. Then they followed him home, which wasn't unusual either.

Dan knew the boys were harassing him so he'd stay away from Annie. It was likely that Stephen hoped if he tormented them enough, there wouldn't be a man alive who would want to be involved with his mother. He was certainly putting forth a good effort, too. But Dan hadn't even mentioned the series of harassments to Annie. Nor had he said anything to anyone else. Dan figured that God knew what He was doing and that God wouldn't suffer him to be tempted beyond that which he was able. And every chance he had, Dan offered to give the boys the gospel. They refused to hear it, of course, but that didn't stop Dan from offering.

November days slipped into snowy, winter December days and snow covered the countryside. School had even been closed for a day because of some severe weather. But that didn't deter Dan and a slew of others from getting together for games of snow-football. Then, on another outing, the entire youth group took a Saturday and went snowmobiling.

However, during the second week of December, Dan was especially busy with putting together the Christmas programs. He was directing one program for the church and another for the school, and because of those commitments, a good amount of his time had to be deferred away from the youth group.

Then one evening, after the first official choir practice, Annie met him at his office.

"I've got good news," she said. "It's answered prayer."

"Well, do tell, Annie," Dan replied with a grin.

She smiled that sweet smile of hers. "Mr. Wells asked me to stop in the office today after I got off of work. I thought Josh was in trouble again." She rolled her eyes, but looked relieved that he obviously wasn't. "Then he told me that Josh did very well on his placement tests, and so he qualifies for a small scholarship."

"That's great, Annie."

"And then," she continued, "Mr. Wells said that an 'anonymous giver' donated five hundred dollars toward Josh's tuition."

At a speculative glance from Annie, Dan shook his head. "Don't look at me, I don't have five hundred dollars."

Annie laughed. "It was Mrs. Engstrom and her daughters," she whispered. "Except I'm not supposed to know. I guessed and then Mr. Wells told me."

"Well, praise the Lord for that, Annie."

She nodded. "I'm praising Him, all right. My tuition bill is paid up until February. . .and after that I should have the insurance money from the things Stephen stole out of the house. You were right. God really is able to take care of me."

"I never had a doubt."

Dan was smiling broadly as he entered his small office. It had been one of those large, walk-in closets, but Pastor Ashford and several members cleaned it out, put a desk in it, hung up some shelves on the walls, and called it Dan's office. And it suited Dan just fine.

Placing several sheets of music on his desk, Dan suddenly had the urge to ask Annie a question that had been lingering in the recesses of his mind since the day he met her.

"Do you sing, Annie?"

"Me?" She looked horrified.

Dan chuckled. "Yes, you. Do you sing?"

She grimaced. "Sort of."

"Will you audition for me?"

"Not a chance!" Annie laughed.

"Oh, come on, Annie. I need another body in the choir, and I'll bet you'd be a second soprano. . .just what I'm looking for."

She paused to consider the idea, so Dan hurried on to convince her.

"I promise I won't make you do a solo or anything. I just need another voice in the choir. Please, Annie? Will you do it?"

She chewed her bottom lip in contemplation, and Dan knew he had her.

"Come on, Annie. Please?"

"Oh, all right. I can carry a tune, I guess."

"That's all I'm asking. And you can probably ride to and from practices with the Winstons."

Annie nodded and Dan smiled. Even though he was busy with the Christmas program, he'd still get to see Annie on a regular basis. Best of all, she'd be a part of his music ministry.

❧

John Winston stood inside his store and looked disbelievingly at the mess that surrounded him. A shattered plate window, groceries thrown everywhere, cash registers smashed on the linoleum floor. Who could have done such a thing?

"We've seen several robberies in this area, John," Sam McDonald, one of the police officers, said. "Vandalism, too. Lots of it."

John shook his head sadly.

"How much money do you think they made off with?"

"None. It's still in the safe," John replied.

Sam nodded. "Probably why they took to vandalizing the place, then. Couldn't get any cash."

John was just sick at the sight of his grocery store in such disarray. Thankfully the inventory had been kept up and, of course, he had insurance. But he'd lose money the next couple of days since he'd have to stay closed to the public to clean up the mess.

John raked a hand through his hair. He was tired, having had his sleep disturbed by a phone call from the police department informing him the alarm was going off at his store. And now, at two in the morning, John had little hope of returning to bed. Maggy, too, was probably up and wondering what was taking so long.

"I guess I had better call my wife," he finally said. "She's probably worried."

Sam nodded. "And we'll check with neighbors and find out if anyone saw or heard anything before the break-in."

"Thanks, Sam."

"You bet."

"I just thank God nobody was hurt."

"That's right. Nobody was hurt."

❧

When Annie arrived at work, she couldn't believe her eyes. "What happened?" she exclaimed.

"Oh, somebody trashed the place," Maggy replied, looking tired and discouraged. "We're going to be closed today, so you've got the option of staying and helping us clean or going home."

"I'll help you clean."

Maggy smiled. "I knew you would, Annie. Thanks. The other girls went home."

Annie nodded. "Where would you like me to begin?"

"It's overwhelming, isn't it?" Maggy agreed. "But why don't you start righting the shelves. Start with the first aisle and move your way across the store."

"All right."

Annie grabbed a broom and headed for Aisle 1, where she

swept up broken glass and placed undamaged goods back on the shelves. It took her two hours to do that one aisle whereas it probably took the intruder less than a minute to do so much damage.

As she moved to Aisle 2, Annie spotted something laying under a cereal box. It caught her eye only because she thought she recognized it. . .and, sure enough. It was one of Deerwood Bible Church's tracts. A wave of anguish poured over her as Annie remembered Dan saying he'd given a tract to Stephen on Thanksgiving Day.

But it could belong to anyone, she silently reasoned. It could even be John or Maggy's. . .and half of Rhinelander has probably gotten one of these at one time or another.

Still, the sorrow in her heart persisted at the thought of Stephen being involved in such a heinous crime. And yet, Annie knew he was capable of it. In fact, she sensed this was, indeed, his doing.

But why? To hurt her more than he already had? To make her lose her job? To hurt the Winstons? But they hadn't done anything to Stephen. And how odd that just weeks ago, he stood in her living room acting rude and overprotective, thinking Dan was going to take his father's place. One minute Stephen is telling me that he hates me, Annie mused, and the next he's telling me to stay away from Dan. What does he care if Dan is a friend or. . .or something more?

Annie suddenly remembered what Dan had once told her. "He doesn't mean he hates you, Annie. It's most likely the drugs talking. Substance abuse, or any addiction, for that matter, almost always causes a person to act schizophrenic."

Drugs. That's what this is really all about, Annie thought, although, until this very moment, she hadn't wanted to admit it. She had always prefaced the notion with a "maybe" or a "perhaps." But, looking at this mess, Annie knew better. The bouts of anger, the mood swings, the rebellious behavior. . .it all pointed to one thing: drug addiction. Annie had read enough to know something about it. Drug habits were expensive, so that would explain the robberies.

But why? she wondered. What started it all? Me? What did I do?

After minutes of musing, it occurred to her that this had all started after Eric's death. Is Stephen angry that he lost his father? she wondered.

Annie thought that could be it. She had been angry for a time, too. Angry that she was left alone to raise and financially support two young sons.

As she continued to straighten shelves, Annie arranged her thoughts as well. Then, finally, with tears in her eyes, she realized what she had to do—she had to talk to John and Maggy. . . and she had to pray that the police would catch up to Stephen before he really hurt himself!

eighteen

Dan finished directing the choir as they sang the final number, "Joy to the World." With an experienced ear, he listened to the basses, tenors, altos, and sopranos, deciding the small ensemble sounded in perfect pitch.

"Okay, that's it for tonight, folks. Thanks for coming. You all did a fine job." Dan smiled as the choir members stretched, talked, or walked off the platform, and he was quite pleased. The dress rehearsal had gone very well. Tomorrow, Saturday night, was the Christmas program, and Dan felt that everyone had done his or her part to prepare. All anybody could do now was trust the Lord to see it all through.

"Good night, Dan," Annie said, walking out of the auditorium with Maggy Winston.

"G'night, Annie," he replied with a smile.

Having Annie in the choir was such a blessing. Even as upset over Stephen as she was, Annie smiled from the middle row and sang as though she felt it coming right from her heart. Dan could see it in her expression. Annie had told him recently that singing in the choir was like good therapy and, after the ordeals she'd suffered with Stephen, just what the doctor ordered. Of course, the Winstons didn't hold Annie responsible for what Stephen might have done to their grocery store. But Dan had recognized the tract as being the same kind he had given Stephen.

John suddenly approached Dan, interrupting his thoughts. "Need some help before we leave?"

Dan shook his head. "Everything can stay as is. But I'm not leaving right away. I need to do some work on a much neglected project."

"Are you still working on that curriculum for next semester?"

Dan nodded. Even if he wasn't around to teach the class on music theory, he wanted the lessons planned out and well organized. Then someone else could easily step in and take his place.

"Hey, what are your plans for Christmas Eve?"

"Well, I only have about fifteen invitations, John," Dan replied with a chuckle, though it was true. "What do you have in mind?"

"Oh, Maggy's folks are coming in for the holiday, and we'd like them to meet you. We've asked Annie and Josh over for Christmas Eve dinner, too. They're getting to be like family. You, too."

"Stop, stop, you're twisting my arm," Dan said without much expression to make it all the funnier. "Okay, I'll come."

John laughed heartily. "That was easy. What about your other fifteen invitations?"

Dan shrugged. "I'll work something out."

John's laughter faded along with his jovial expression. "Maggy and I don't mean to hoard your fellowship, Dan. We understand that there are others who want time with you before you leave. It's just that, well, there's a special friendship between all of us. . .you and Annie and Maggy and me."

Dan pursed his lips in thought. The "you and Annie" part made him unsure, yet again, that he could leave her behind; however, the situation with Stephen made it impossible to take her along—even if she did agree to marry him, which posed its own dilemma. What if Annie didn't want to get married again? What if she didn't want to marry him? Dan suspected that Annie had special feelings for him, too, but they'd never discussed it, and it needed to be. . .if he was staying. . .or leaving. Either way. And around and around his thoughts went.

"Did I offend you, Dan?" John asked, looking concerned as they headed out of the auditorium. "You got kind of quiet."

"No, I was just preoccupied with my thoughts. . .and, yes, I'll come on Christmas Eve. Wild horses couldn't keep me away, John."

"Well, that's good," he replied with a puzzled frown. "I guess that's good?"

"I don't know what it is," Dan confessed with a slow grin. "But good or bad, right or wrong, I promised myself I wouldn't make any decisions until after the Christmas program. That's enough stress for the time being."

"I hear you!" John agreed, though he still looked puzzled. Then he lowered his voice to just above a whisper. "Are you thinking about staying, Dan?"

They were in the vestibule now. "Yeah, I'm thinking about it," Dan drawled lazily. "But please don't say anything just yet. I don't want to get Ann—" He managed to stop himself just before divulging more than he wished for now. "I don't want to get anybody's hopes up," he finished in a practical tone of voice.

"I understand," John replied, grinning from ear to ear. "I won't start rejoicing just yet, but I will keep praying."

"I'm counting on it."

They parted, then, John leaving for home and Dan heading for the quiet of his office to finish his paperwork, which had been piling up for an entire week.

Hours later, Dan glanced at his watch and grimaced. It was nearly 2:00 A.M. Stretching, Dan shuffled some papers on his desk and moved them off to the side. He'd have to finish up next week. The more Dan worked on this curriculum, the more excited he got about it. There were plenty of kids in this school who loved good, God-honoring music enough to learn the basics of it—and that really thrilled Dan. It disappointed him to think he might not get to teach the class.

So I stay for another six months, he mused. That would work. . .and, after that I could decide whether to leave or stay in Rhinelander for good. . .

The hole in that idea, Dan suddenly realized, was that Mike Pettit would need another evangelist to take over the music aspect of his ministry. Mike had already been without someone for six months, and he had made it clear during their last phone conversation that he was anxious to get Dan back.

So I've come back around to the same old question, Dan thought tumultuously. Do I go or do I stay?

Pushing the chair away from the desk, Dan stood and prepared to leave for his apartment. He grabbed his jacket from where it hung on a hanger on the back of the door. Then, after a final inspection of his desk to make sure he hadn't forgotten anything, Dan flicked off the light. He turned sharply and at that very moment, he ran right into Stephen Fetherston.

"What in the world. . .?"

"Don't you ever look where you're going?" Stephen shot at him.

"It's two o'clock in the morning. I thought I was the only one here." Dan narrowed his gaze. "You should be home in bed."

"Ditto. Don't you holy rollers ever sleep?"

Dan sighed. He was exhausted, and the last thing he felt like doing was exchanging glib remarks with a juvenile delinquent. "What can I do for you, Stephen?" he finally asked.

"I've got a question for you."

"Fire away."

"Yeah, well, I think we should talk in your office. You've got a nice little office, too. I've been in it quite a few times, as a matter of fact. . .only you weren't around." Stephen chortled. "Somebody ought to warn you guys to lock up your church at night."

Dan fought to overcome his rising irritation. He reminded himself to be thankful that Stephen and his friends hadn't ransacked the place.

"Me and my friends have made a habit of sleeping in the church on especially cold nights. Those pews ain't all that uncomfortable, either. You might want to tell the good pastor that so he can get a good alarm system."

"This is a place of worship, Stephen," Dan replied, struggling to keep the exhaustion out of his voice. "Pastor Ashford decided these doors should never be locked. And you've probably noticed that there isn't much to steal around here. No computers or high-tech phone systems. In fact, much of our equipment is outdated and not worth anything to anyone but us here at Deerwood Bible."

"Tell me about it," the young man remarked in a sarcastic tone. "Except. . .we did find ten bucks in somebody's desk drawer."

Dan forced himself not to react. He sensed it was what Stephen was looking for—a reaction.

Dan turned on the light and reentered his office. "Have a seat," he told Stephen, indicating the desk chair. Then Dan sat down on the corner of his desktop. "Now what's this question you wanted to ask me?"

Stephen copped a belligerent expression. "If God is so good and all that, then why did He let my dad die in a truck accident, huh? I mean, I read that thing you gave me, but I don't know that God loves the world all that much."

Dan had to smile. This was the opportunity he'd been praying for! True, it hadn't come along when he had wanted it to come along; however, God still provided it.

"Stephen," he began, "it's true that God allows trials in our life, but it's Satan who owns death and mortal destruction. In that tract I gave you, it says that the wages of sin is death and we just happen to be living in a sin-cursed world. Everyone of us is going to die at some time. But we have to make the decision now: Are we going to die and face eternal death, the second death? Or are we going to live forever with the Savior, Jesus Christ?"

Stephen just sat there as if absorbing everything he just heard. He didn't appear to be looking at anything in particular; he was just staring at something in the distance.

"So, what do you think?" Dan finally prompted.

Stephen's dark brown eyes came back and obstinately held Dan's gaze. "I didn't want my dad to die. I think it was real unfair of God. . .or Satan. . .or whoever to let him die!"

Dan nodded. "I'm sure it seems that way."

Stephen stood. "And that's the way it is, man."

Dan sensed he should back off right here. No sense in shoving the gospel down the kid's throat. One had to accept God's gift of salvation—it couldn't be forced.

"Okay, now let me ask you a question. Only fair."

Stephen shrugged.

"Did you break into Paradigm Foods?"

"Yep."

"Hmm. . .your mom suspected you did. She found the tract I gave you on the floor."

"I threw it there on purpose," Stephen admitted rebelliously. "I had no need for it."

"Well, I suppose the best thing for you to do is to turn yourself in to the police."

Stephen laughed. "Like, right. I'll do it right now."

"I've got to call them, Stephen. What you did was against the law."

"Go ahead. Call the police. I'll be gone before they get here anyhow."

Dan picked up the telephone.

"But let me ask you one more thing, Holy Joe," Stephen said tauntingly.

Dan paused before dialing the police department. "All right."

A muscle worked in Stephen's jaw. "You planning to marry my mom?"

"I'm thinking about it."

At the reply, Stephen became enraged and lunged at Dan with his fists balled. But before he could throw a punch, Dan had dropped the telephone receiver and pinned Stephen to the wall.

"You can't control your mom, Stephen," Dan told him in a low, hard tone, "and you can't control me. You can't control what happened to your dad and. . .you can't even control yourself at the moment!" Dan softened his voice. "You need God and His controlling Holy Spirit in your life. Without it, I hate to even think what's going to happen to you."

Stephen twisted out of Dan's grasp and made for the door. He glared at Dan, but he didn't say anything else. Then he turned and ran through the hallway. Dan followed and watched him leave the building. Then he called the police.

❧

The Christmas program began with Dan playing "O Holy Night" on the piano. Then four members of the congregation did a dramatic reading about the birth of Christ. Next the choir sang "What Child Is This?" and afterwards Lisa Johnson played a solo, "The First Noel," on her flute. JoAnn Farley then read a touching Christmas poem that she wrote while Dan played "I Wonder As I Wander" in the background. There wasn't a dry eye in the house. Pastor Ashford took the pulpit then and delivered a Christmas message, which was followed by the finale.

As the choir members took their places on the platform in front of the pulpit, Dan introduced the medley they would be singing. The auditorium was packed to its limit tonight, but somehow Dan managed to spot Stephen sitting in the farthest pew back. He met the young man's dark gaze, puzzled by his appearance; however, not even missing a syllable, Dan continued with his introduction.

Turning to direct the choir then, Dan's gaze met Annie's. She didn't appear disturbed in the least, smiling as she was, and Dan could only hope that she wouldn't see Stephen. Annie had been quite upset when she learned about the confrontation that took place in the wee hours of the morning and it would be very embarrassing for her if she got upset right now. But Annie kept her gaze on him, her conductor, just as she and all the choir members had been instructed to do.

Finally, at the program's conclusion, the audience was asked to stand and join the choir in singing "Joy to the World." Then the program ended and the auditorium's lights were turned up.

Dan looked out over the swarms of people gathering in the aisles, but Stephen wasn't among them. Dan couldn't help but wonder how much Stephen had taken in.

He's searching, Dan realized. *He wants to know the Truth, and as long as Stephen continues to seek he'll find.*

"Nice job, Mr. Brenshaw."

Dan turned and saw Annie's friend, Charlene. "Well, thank you, Mrs. Hughes."

"Annie said I wouldn't be disappointed and I wasn't."

Dan smiled. "Glad to hear it."

Then Josh was standing right beside him. "Did you think it was better than our school's program?" he asked Charlene.

She smiled. "Oh, I'd say they were about a tie." Then she looked at Dan. "I don't think I've ever attended two Christmas programs in one year. Really gets you in the mood, though, doesn't it?"

"That's the whole idea," Dan replied.

And then it occurred to him that there was a lot of work to do in this small northern town of Rhinelander. There were dozens of Charlenes out there who needed to be reached. There were, most likely, an equal amount of Stephens who were headed for destruction and needed the Savior. And there was one young man named Josh who could probably use a father-figure. And then, of course, there was Annie.

Looking at Josh now, Dan gave him a playful elbow to the ribs. "Go get your mom, buddy, and let's go out for pizza."

Josh's face lit up like a shining star. "That'd be awesome. I'll be right back!"

Watching the boy weave his way through the crowd, Dan could only smile in his wake.

nineteen

The pizza outing included more than just Annie, Dan, and Josh. The Winstons and their three children came along to the restaurant as well as Billy Smith and his mother. . .and even Charlene agreed to join them. They took up four tables, all pushed together in the middle of the dining room. Above the din of the other patrons, including those at their own table, separate conversations ensued. Charlene and Mrs. Smith seemed to have a lot in common, Josh and Billy decided to play some video games in the outer lobby, and the Winstons were talking between themselves at one end of the table. At the other end, Dan and Annie were carrying on their own conversation.

"I'm glad you talked me into singing with the choir, Dan," Annie told him with a smile. "I enjoyed it, and I think the Christmas program was a great success."

Dan nodded. "It's rewarding to have a part in something like that, isn't it?"

Now it was Annie's turn to nod.

"Stephen was there. Did you see him?"

Annie's jaw dropped slightly. "He was there? Where?"

Dan grinned. "I didn't think you saw him. He was sitting in one of the back pews."

"Stephen?" Annie could hardly believe it.

But Dan was nodding. "He was there, but he left early. . .maybe during the finale."

"Oh, my word! Do you think he meant to cause trouble?"

"I don't know. Maybe he wanted to intimidate me, or maybe he wanted to see his mom in the choir." Dan smiled. "But I'm encouraged, Annie. Stephen came to church on his own accord and he most likely heard the gospel again."

Now Annie had to smile. "Stephen was probably shocked when he saw me. I've never been part of anything like that before. Too busy, I guess." She shrugged. "And I'm just as

153

busy as I always was, really, but somehow I have extra time. It's amazing."

"God's timetable always is," Dan agreed.

Then Dan told Annie about Stephen and his friends following him. "It's been happening since Thanksgiving Day, Annie," he said. "I wasn't going to tell you, but I think that after last night and tonight you ought to know."

Annie wasn't sure whether to feel embarrassed or irritated with her son. "Stephen is an angry young man," she finally said with a heavy heart. "I'm sorry—"

"Don't be sorry, Annie," Dan replied sincerely. "Stephen's bad decisions aren't your fault. And there's a reason for this, I'm sure. Besides, the harassment has tapered off some. I guess this is just something between Stephen and me now." Dan chuckled. "Actually, it's between Stephen and God, even if it might look like it involves me. But just as David said of his fighting Goliath, 'The battle is the Lord's'." Lifting a knowing brow, Dan added, "That's in 1 Samuel 17."

Annie wrote the passage down on a white paper napkin and then slipped it into her purse. Then she looked back at Dan, who gave her a warm smile that threatened to melt her heart.

A moment of weighted silence passed between them before Dan spoke again. "Mind if I ask you a personal question?"

"Oh, I always mind," Annie teased him, "but I usually answer your questions anyway."

"Yeah, usually."

Annie chuckled softly. "Ask away, Dan."

He paused as if choosing his words carefully. "Do you think you'd ever get married again, Annie?"

His expression was one of seriousness, but she shook her head at him anyway. "Your questions, Dan, never cease to amaze me."

"Too personal?"

"Sort of." Annie sipped her cola and then set it back down on the table. "But I guess I should be used to it by now, huh?"

"Quit stalling," he teased her.

Annie rolled her eyes. But, as her sense of humor faded away, she somehow found the courage to look Dan full in the face before answering his question. "Yes, I'd get married again," she began softly. "If the right man asked me, that is," she added, meaning him, of course. Annie figured the remark was lost on Dan—he only thought of her as a friend. . .a friend like John Winston.

Annie noticed, then, that Dan was nodding his head slightly as he digested her reply, and suddenly she felt a tremendous desire to share her feelings. . .at least some of them.

"Now, can I tell you something personal, Dan?"

"Sure can." Stretching his arm across the back of her chair, he gave her his undivided attention. "Go ahead."

Annie considered him, his sharp, teal eyes shining into hers beneath the dim lights of the restaurant. Her heart ached, but she sensed that she would find some relief in being honest.

"I'm going to miss you when you leave," she murmured. She longed to say more, but just didn't know how to bring the words up from her heart to her lips.

Then Dan looked momentarily thoughtful, and for what seemed like a good long minute, he said nothing. Annie wondered what was going through his mind—his expression gave not a single clue. Yes, he had warned her that he was leaving. Yes, that meant she shouldn't have allowed herself to feel too much for him. And yet, Dan didn't seem angry or sad or troubled in the least. Dan just seemed pensive—but in a resigned sort of way.

Finally, he looked into her eyes and said, "Annie, I don't guess I'm going anywhere this January."

Stunned, she lifted questioning brows.

Dan grinned. "You heard me. There's nothing wrong with your ears."

"You're staying. . .here in Rhinelander?"

"I'm staying."

Annie was suddenly smiling so broadly that her face hurt, and if they weren't in the restaurant, she thought she'd like to throw her arms around his neck for joy! However, the entire table was looking over at them now and wearing expressions of curious expectancy.

"What's that, Dan?" John Winston called from the other end of the table. A mischievous smile curved his lips. "I was sure that I just heard Annie say something about you staying in Rhinelander."

Annie felt her face flame with embarrassment. She hadn't meant to be so loud about it.

Dan gave her a reassuring wink and then looked at John. "You heard right. Rhinelander is my new home until I get further marching orders from my Commander, Jesus Christ." Several people chuckled at Dan's remark.

"So I can start rejoicing, huh, Dan?"

"Go right ahead, John," he replied. "I'll rejoice with you."

So will I, Annie thought as something wondrous enveloped her. It was such a feeling of joy that it nearly made her giddy. What a miracle! Dan was staying!

❧

"I just knew Dan was going to stay," Maggy stated as John lit a fire in the fireplace on Christmas Eve.

"Well, then, you had more faith than I did," he replied over his shoulder. "I was pretty certain that Dan was going to leave and that Annie was going to be hurt."

"So you think there's something between them? Is Annie the reason Dan is staying? I mean, it is kind of obvious."

"Annie's part of the reason, for sure. Maybe she's even most of the reason." He grinned mischievously at his wife. "And I know something you don't know," he said in a singsong voice that sounded much like their children when they teased each other.

Maggy drew her chin back. "What do you know that I don't know?"

"Can't tell."

"John Matthew Winston, you spill the beans right now!"

"No can do. I've been sworn to secrecy."

Maggy placed indignant fists upon her hips. "That's not nice to tease me, John. Now you've got to tell me."

"All right. Since we're 'one flesh' and all that. . ."

He chuckled and rose from where he had been kneeling by the fireplace. A warm, golden glow filled the room now as the flames began to consume the kindling. Walking over to where Maggy stood by the doorway, John slipped his arms around her waist. Then he kissed her.

"You're under the mistletoe, you know."

Maggy batted her lashes in mock innocence. "I am? Imagine that."

After another kiss, John pulled back slightly. "Dan said he's planning to ask Annie to marry him tonight. Isn't that nice? On Christmas Eve?"

Maggy gasped with pleasure. "He must have told his family, then."

John nodded. "Dan said his folks are thrilled with the idea of his engagement. They gave him the 'go ahead,' even though they haven't met Annie. His parents said they trust his judgment, but they're excited to meet Annie, too."

"How wonderful!" But then a concerned frown suddenly replaced Maggy's smile. "I just hope Dan has got sense enough to propose in private. I mean, if Dan does it in front of all of us, Annie will die of embarrassment!"

John smiled. "Yeah, well, you know Dan. . .and Annie had better get used to it." He laughed.

Maggy sighed, looking utterly delighted once again. "Dan's decision to stay in Rhinelander is answered prayer, isn't it? For us, for Annie, and all of Deerwood Bible Church. God is good."

Smiling broadly now, Maggy nodded. "Yes, He is."

Just then, Maggy's mother stepped into the room. Seeing the couple, still embraced in each other's arms, she rolled her eyes and looked a bit embarrassed. "I just used the last diaper, Maggy. Have you got more stashed somewhere that I don't know about?"

"The last diaper?" Maggy frowned in confusion, looking from her mother to her husband. And then, it seemed, she remembered. . .

"Oh, John, I forgot to buy disposable diapers this afternoon when I was at the store! I would have had enough except Noah had a bit of the flu a couple of days ago."

John sighed in resignation as his arms fell from Maggy's waist. "Okay, I'll make a quick run to the store. Need anything else while I'm going?"

Maggy and her mother did a double check in the kitchen just as the front doorbell rang. John answered it, welcoming Dan, Annie, and Josh into the house.

"I've got to make a quick run to the store, but Maggy and her parents are here. . .and the kids, of course. So have a seat in the living room where it's warm. I'll be back shortly."

Dan helped Annie off with her coat and handed it to John, who hung it in the front hall closet. Next came Josh's and then Dan's.

"Want some company on this journey of yours?" Dan offered on a teasing note.

John grinned and shook his head. Then he pulled on his ski jacket. "This is going to be one of those quick, but necessary journeys. I'm going for diapers."

Dan chuckled.

"Hey, listen, this could be you next year, pal," John teased him right back.

Dan immediately sobered, his eyebrows raised in surprise, and John laughed all the way to his mini-van.

Driving to the store, John listened to a cassette tape of various Christmas music. His spirits were high, anticipating a wonderful evening ahead with his family and friends. Maybe I'll talk Dan into playing the piano for us, he mused. The girls can play their violins. And then I'll get out my Bible and read Isaiah 9:6 and then Luke, Chapter 2.

John was still engrossed in his thoughts as he parked the mini-van in front of his store, climbed out, and then walked to the door. The keys on his key chain jangled together as he found the right one to, first, shut off the alarm and a second one to unlock the door. It was a process born out of daily habit.

Then suddenly John startled as something cold and hard was stuck in the back of his neck. Turning ever so slowly, John saw two boys behind him. One was unmistakably Stephen Fetherston, and the other John didn't recognize, but he was holding a shotgun directly under John's chin.

"Merry Christmas, Mr. Paradigm Foods," the young man holding the gun said. "It's so nice of you to open up your store for us and let us pick out our presents." He laughed. "Ain't that right, Steve?"

John glanced at Stephen, whose expression seemed as indifferent as the night was cold. Stephen's friend, however, didn't seem to notice or care.

"We started off following that holy roller tonight, since he went and picked up Steve's mom. . .even after we told him not to. And then, wouldn't you know, while we were just trying to decide what his punishment should be, you come walking out of the house. Didn't take much brains to figure that you were coming to your store. At least that's what we were banking on." Again the boy laughed. "Get it? We were banking on it?"

His mood changed abruptly and he shoved the gun at John. "Open the door. We want what we came to get the first time—the money in your safe."

Turning back around, John pushed the door open and led the boys into the store. It was dark except for a few night-lights that were left on, ironically, in case of a theft.

"Open the safe," the boy with the gun ordered, steering John with a nudge of the shotgun.

John complied, wondering if the gun was loaded. He wondered if the boy holding it was a farm kid and knew how to use it, or if he was a city kid just pretending. Was this a bluff? And, if it was, would he get himself killed by calling it?

"Open the safe," the boy ordered again.

As John's fingers touched the large, combination lock, he suddenly got the notion that he was a dead man either way. He had heard of an account where a shop owner was killed and locked up in his own safe after a robbery. Was that what would happen here tonight? And, if so, wouldn't it be better to save the money for Maggy and the kids. . .if he was going to heaven tonight, regardless?

Turning slowly, John faced his assailants. "I won't open it." He spoke in a matter-of-fact tone, one devoid of any sort of challenge. True, he was calling the kids' bluff, which was dangerous and maybe even stupid. Nonetheless, John really believed the end result would be the same whether he opened the safe or not.

"I'm going to kill you, man," the boy threatened, "so you'd better open it up and do it fast!"

John shook his head as thoughts of Maggy and his children flitted through his mind. *Lord God,* he prayed silently, *please look after them. . .keep them safe. . .provide for them. . .and I know You will if Your perfect plan is to take me home. . .*

The kid cocked the shotgun and suddenly Stephen spoke up.

"Put it away, Ed," he told his friend. "Robbery is one thing, man, but I don't want any part of murder."

"I knew you'd chicken out," he sneered. "You ain't been fun for weeks. What's a matter with you, anyhow?"

"Just put the gun away, Ed," Stephen replied, all the while sounding surprisingly calm. "We can go rob that convenience store down the street. There's just one clerk in there, and I know her from high school. She's real dumb. She'll give us whatever we want."

"Yeah, and last time we did that, we only got $50. Ain't no money in those convenience stores."

"Just put the gun away, okay? I can't think when you've got that thing cocked."

"You can't think anyway!"

Ed hoisted the shotgun up to his shoulder again. "One last chance, Mr. Paradigm Foods. Then I—"

At that very moment, Stephen lunged toward Ed, knocking the gun askew. It went off, shattering the glass door of a cooler near the frozen foods section. John immediately took the opportunity to make a run for it to the back of the store. Shaking unbelievably, he phoned the police from the extension behind the meat department. Then he went into the basement and hid near the receiving area, feeling like a coward and yet thankful to be alive.

Another shot resounded from above him. John heard it clearly. Then another. Oh, Lord, don't let those kids kill themselves, he muttered in prayer. I'd rather they shoot up my store than die.

Silence ensued for the next fifteen minutes, after which John gathered the courage to venture out from where he'd been hiding. His heart hammered as he walked up the basement stairs, unsure of what would meet him around the corner. When nothing did, he made his way through the meat department and finally down the produce aisle. In the distance, near the front doors, he saw a police officer and breathed a sigh of relief. Through the plate glass windows, he saw the red flashing lights from their patrol cars and decided it was the best sight he'd ever seen.

However, the next sight sickened him. It was Stephen Fetherston, lying face down on the floor as a tiny stream of blood trickled out from beneath him. Stephen had been shot!

twenty

Annie stood at the far end of the waiting room feeling as though her world had crashed down around her and now lay at her feet in sharp, fragmented pieces. It wasn't the first time she had felt this way, either. The first time was after Eric died, and back then just as now, she felt very alone and very scared.

With her arms folded tightly across her chest, Annie closed her eyes and prayed that Stephen would survive the surgery he was currently undergoing. The doctors said it was a miracle that he had even survived the ride to Rhinelander's hospital, what with a gunshot wound to the chest.

Annie's knees felt weak as she thought of Stephen with such a horrible injury. He was a lot of things, but he was still her son, her child, and Annie hurt for him. She hurt with him.

Then suddenly she felt a hand on her shoulder and looked to find Dan standing beside her.

"You want a cup of coffee?"

Annie shook her head and looked away. She folded her arms even tighter.

"C'mon, Annie. Come and sit down. You've been standing here for an hour."

Again, she shook her head.

"And will you talk to me already?" Dan asked softly. "Don't go hiding inside yourself, Annie. Let me help you through this."

She looked at him, wanting so desperately to depend on him right now.

"God wants us to bear one another's burdens, Annie. You're not alone in this. Let me help carry the weight."

Annie slowly turned away again. Dan was saying everything she longed to hear, and yet she didn't know how to reply. Always in the past, she had been the one left to pick up life's pieces, and she just didn't have the strength to do it anymore.

"Annie, look at me," Dan said earnestly.

Slowly, she turned toward him, and when her eyes met his, so full of compassion, Annie suddenly broke down and wept into the palms of her hands.

She heard Dan sigh and then he pulled her into his arms. "Well, I guess that's better," he said. "I was getting kind of worried. You've been like some china doll in a store window ever since the police came to the Winstons' house and gave us the news."

Pulling back slightly, he handed her a tissue, and Annie wiped her eyes. That did little good, because the tears kept coming and coming. Dan still held her in a comforting embrace. The touch of a loved one. . .well, it helped.

"I. . .I'm s-sorry to have r-ruined Christmas Eve," Annie finally choked out.

"Will you stop it? You didn't ruin anything. And we've had this conversation before, Annie. Guilt is not of God."

She nodded a weak reply. "I believe that, but somehow I feel. . .embarrassed and humiliated over what Stephen did tonight." Annie sniffled. "On top of that, I'm ashamed of myself for. . .for feeling that way when Stephen might. . .die."

"Beating yourself up good, huh? Think it'll help the situation?"

Lifting her head, Annie glared at him for speaking to her so harshly. But then his words slowly met their mark, and Annie knew he was right. Feeling guilty wouldn't help Stephen right now. And if guilt wasn't of God, she had to somehow let it go.

"Okay, point taken," she said, gulping back a fresh onset of tears.

Dan smiled gently. "Good. And now I think you need to talk to the Winstons. This has been upsetting for them, too. And, like me, they feel you're shutting them out. . .except they don't know why."

"It's nothing personal, Dan. It just. . .hurts."

"And so we'll all hurt together, okay?"

"But. . .what if. . ."

Before Annie could finish asking her question, Dan was leading her through the waiting room. John and Maggy were sitting in hard-back chairs placed up against the wall. They sat side-by-side, wearing grave expressions.

Annie's tears came again at the sight of them. "I-I'm s-so sorry," she said. An apology was all she could manage.

Maggy smiled and rose from her chair to put her arms around Annie. She held her like a sister. "It's okay, Annie. It wasn't you who robbed the store. And, as for Stephen. Well, we have forgiven him."

"Th-thank you," Annie sobbed against Maggy's forest green velvet Christmas dress. Somehow airing the wound, though it stung at first, lessened the pain.

After a few minutes, Annie pulled back and dried away her tears. She looked over at John, then. He was her employer and yet he was her friend—still her friend, in spite of what her son had done.

"Thanks for riding in the ambulance with Stephen," she told him.

John gave her a tender smile. "I wouldn't have it any other way, Annie." Then he stood up and stretched. "You know, Stephen saved my life. He tried to convince the other boy to put the gun away. He even suggested they leave the store. I sort of got the feeling that he didn't want to be part of the robbery in the first place. And I'm extremely thankful that the police caught those other two boys. But Stephen. . ." John raised his brows as if to make a point. "Stephen is beginning to have a change of heart, I think."

"Getting tired of living like some modern-day outlaw," Dan added with a wry grin.

John agreed.

"Oh, I want to believe that so much!" Annie replied fervently. As her emotions returned to some semblance of normality, she looked back at Dan. Then she gave him a grateful smile for being there when she needed him.

"Do you think Josh is okay?" she finally managed to ask.

He nodded. "But I'm sure he's as anxious to know about Stephen as we are. So as soon as we hear something, one of us will call."

Josh had been ordered, despite his protests, to stay at the Winstons' house while Annie, Dan, and Maggy went to the hospital.

"Maggy's father will keep him occupied," John added. "He

likes kids. . .and he loves a good chess game. My guess is that he'll have Josh playing in no time."

"Thanks you, guys," Annie murmured as tears of gratitude began to fall. "I was feeling so alone."

"Annie, let's all pray," Dan suggested.

She nodded and so, in a small, close group, the four friends held hands. Each took a turn praying for Stephen, and Annie noticed that Dan, John, and Maggy used various verses from the Bible when they prayed. "Claiming God's promises," Maggy had once told their Bible study class when they discussed prayer on a Sunday morning. Annie had never heard it done before, nor had she ever experienced such a sense of God's power while in prayer. Hers had been limp requests compared to the power these Christians possessed, and Annie realized it was all because they knew God's Word and believed it!

Finally her turn to pray came, and Annie was suddenly reminded of the part in the Bible where Jesus talked about having faith as a grain of mustard seed. It had been a passage of Scripture that spoke to Annie's heart immediately. Even a faith so small was still mountain-moving faith—and on that promise, she built her prayer for Stephen.

After they finished praying, Dan and John went to the cafeteria for coffee, but it wasn't until the wee hours of the morning that the surgeon came out to speak to them about Stephen.

"Would you like to talk in private, Mrs. Fetherston?" the doctor asked.

Annie shook her head. "These are my friends, and they're as close as family members. It's okay."

He nodded curtly. "Your son survived the surgery, but we almost lost him once during the operation. He's in critical condition. Eventually, we'd like to transfer him to Children's Hospital of Wisconsin, which is located in Milwaukee, but we'll have to wait until his vital signs are stable. It's going to be touch and go for the next twelve hours. I'm sorry I don't have better news for you."

Leaving the waiting room, the doctor promised to keep in touch. "Oh, and if you'd like to see him, Mrs. Fetherston," he added, "I'll have one of the nurses come and get you as soon as your son is admitted to the intensive care unit. But I'm afraid your friends will have to wait here."

Annie nodded. "Yes, I'd like to see him as soon as I can."

≈

John and Maggy decided to go home a while later, but they made Annie promise to telephone if Stephen's condition changed.

"And what about you, Dan?" she asked once they were alone in the hospital's waiting room. "Don't you want to go home and get some sleep?"

"Annie," he replied, "I wouldn't dream of leaving you at a time like this."

Lowering her chin, Annie smiled demurely. She thought that all of Dan's "personal questions," genuine concern, and tender assurances were only endearing him to her and causing her to fall deeper in love with him. Looking back at Dan, she wondered if he would welcome her love one day or if a romantic involvement was something he was really trying to avoid.

Then, just as Annie was about to question Dan's motives, the nurse appeared.

"Mrs. Fetherston? I can take you to the ICU now to see your son."

Annie stood and followed the nurse down one corridor and then another. Once inside the ICU, Annie was escorted to Stephen's bedside. Much to her horror, plastic tubes, like streamers, were everywhere—coming out of his arms, his nose, and one particularly large piece of blue tubing was coming from Stephen's mouth. A machine was beeping in a rhythmic pattern while another hissed as it pumped fluid from a hanging bag to Stephen's battered-looking body.

"He is breathing on his own, but we've got him on a respirator as a precaution. It's a fairly typical procedure, especially after the kind of surgery your son had."

Annie nodded, glad that the nurse had taken time to explain things to her. It was terribly hard to see Stephen in this condition, and Annie decided it was because of God and Him alone that she could bear it.

The nurse motioned Annie forward. "He's sedated," she said, "and it's nearly time for his next dose of medicine. But you can talk to him. He can hear you. He's been in and out of consciousness for the last fifteen minutes."

Annie leaned over the bed and touched Stephen's forehead. It was cool and dry. She stroked his dark hair. "Stephen? Stephen, can you hear me?"

His eyelids fluttered and then opened, revealing groggy brown eyes, but Annie saw a spark of recognition come to light in them.

She smiled. "You're going to be all right, Stephen," she said with a confidence that surprised even herself. "We've been praying. . .the Winstons, Dan, and I. . .and. . .I love you, Stephen."

His dark eyes pooled with unshed tears. He tried to speak, but the respirator prevented any sound from coming forth. Then he tried to fight it.

"Easy now, Stephen," the nurse told him as she monitored one machine and then another.

"It's all right, Stephen," Annie told him soothingly. "Just do what the nurse tells you so you get better, okay?"

Stephen replied with his eyes, blinking once, like an affirmative nod. Next, he seemed to struggle as he pulled his left hand out from under the thin flannel blanket that covered the lower half of his body. It was his only free hand, since the other held an IV needle.

His eyes locked with Annie's then, as if beseeching her to take it. She did, and Stephen held on with an amazingly strong grip, considering his condition. Bringing his hand up to her cheek, Annie stroked his forearm for several long moments. It was as close to an embrace as she dared, given the surrounding equipment.

Stephen grew sleepier as the nurse applied his medication intravenously, but still he hung onto his mother's hand. It reminded Annie of when she used to sit at his bedside when Stephen was little and afraid of the dark. He had wanted her to hold his hand then, too.

Leaning over, Annie kissed his forehead, and suddenly Stephen wasn't that horrible, rebellious, dangerous young man. Suddenly he was her little boy again!

❧

Dan stood as Annie reentered the waiting room. His eyes were narrowed in a kind of intense concern. "How is he?"

Annie smiled. "I really believe he's going to be all right, Dan," she replied. She sat down in the chair next to his. "He wanted me to hold his hand, and then I experienced a real sense of peace."

Taking his seat again, Dan smiled, too. "That's nice, Annie."

"And that hard look in Stephen's eyes was gone," she continued. Then she sighed a long, tired breath. "But I know it's not over yet. There will be court appearances in our future, and Stephen may or may not get sent to that lock-in school."

"Something to pray about," Dan remarked lazily, as he rested his head back against the wall.

"What time is it?"

Dan looked at his watch. "Almost 4:00 A.M." He chuckled. "Merry Christmas, Annie."

"Merry Christmas, Dan." Then she chuckled also. "You know, it was certainly nice of God to give me the best Christmas present ever—I got my son back, Dan. I know I did. It took something as terrible as this night, but I've got him back. And with God's help, I'm never going to let him go!"

"Amen!"

Annie smiled and a comfortable silence settled down around them as they sat in the brightly lit waiting area. Chairs aligned the walls with two rows set up to make an aisle in the center. Large, square tables were scattered about, bearing a barrage of magazines.

Annie closed her eyes, and a sweet-sounding melody began to play in her head. "I'm remembering that piece of music you wrote, Dan," she said, suddenly wanting to share it with him. "It has a tranquil effect on me, too. . .as if reaffirming that everything is going to be all right."

Dan smiled. "A song in the night, huh? Right out of the Book of Job."

Annie didn't know the Book of Job very well, but it wasn't the first time someone had made reference to it when considering her circumstances. Guess I'd better read it, she mused.

"You know, I thought of a title for that melody you're talking about," Dan said.

"Really? What did you come up with?"

Dan lolled his head toward her and then smiled into her

eyes. "I've called it 'Annie's Song'."

For a good long moment, Annie sat there in a stunned silence. When finally she found her voice, she said, "I never had anyone name a song for me."

"Well, it's your song, Annie," Dan replied. "So it just had to be 'Annie's Song'."

Tears welled in her eyes and then spilled onto her cheeks.

"Oh, now don't cry." Dan made a hasty move for the box of tissues on the table to his right. He set it in her lap.

Pulling out one tissue, then another, Annie dabbed her eyes. "I'm so touched, Dan, I don't even know what to say. . . oh, yes, I do." On impulse she leaned over and kissed his cheek. "I love you, Dan."

"I love you, too, Annie."

She blinked. "You do?"

"Well, sure I do. You think I'd talk just any woman into singing in the choir?"

Annie shrugged.

"And do you think I'd impose myself on just anybody the way I've imposed on you?"

She laughed through her tears.

Then, reaching over to where his suit jacket lay on the chair to his right, Dan pulled a small velveteen-covered box from the front pocket. "This isn't quite the way I had planned all this, Annie, but it seems the time is right. . ."

Annie opened the box and peered at the slim silver-banded ring. Its tiny diamond seemed to wink at her affectionately.

"Will you marry me, Annie?"

"Oh, Dan. . ."

"I know it's not much, Annie," he said of the ring as she slipped it on her finger, "and I'll try to do better when I buy the wedding set."

"It's perfect," Annie replied.

"I'll probably never be rich."

"I don't care about being rich." More tears filled her eyes, and Annie was glad for the tissue box still resting in her lap. "I can't believe that you want to marry me, Dan. I mean, I'm a country bumpkin who never even finished high school."

"Listen, Annie, I know some people with their doctorates

who aren't half as intelligent as you are."

"You're so sweet."

"Thanks. So. . .what do you say? Should we get married this week or next?"

Annie lifted a brow. "What happened to courtship?" She paused, momentarily pensive. "Oh, I guess we're past the courtship part of a relationship, aren't we? But how about an engagement?"

Dan brought his chin back, looking surprised. "Well, Annie, we're going to have an engagement," he promised her. "But a week or two is plenty long enough, don't you think?"

Annie had to force herself not to laugh, to even smirk. Dan was serious! He was as impetuous as the apostle Peter. . .and she was just going to have to learn to live with it.

"I love you, Dan," she said once more. "And whenever you want to get married is fine with me."

"Well, good. I thought maybe you were going to turn me down for a minute there."

"Are you kidding? I wouldn't dare!"

They shared a laugh.

"I'll have you know," Dan continued, "that my parents are excited at the mere prospect of my getting married. Dad says it's been a long time coming, and I can tell that Mom loves you already. I've told her all about you, and now Mom's got big plans for our wedding, so consider yourself fairly warned."

Dan shook his head then, as if in wonder, and Annie remembered that marriage hadn't ever been part of his future plans—not since coming to Rhinelander, anyway.

"Are you sure you want to do this?" Annie couldn't help but ask. "You sure you want to get married?"

Dan's eyes, teal blue with a warm glow of sincerity, met her questioning gaze. "I'm as sure of marrying you as I am of anything. I'm in love with you, Annie. No doubt about it."

"Oh, Dan. . ."

And despite the hospital setting, her exhaustion, and everything that had happened in the past ten hours, Annie never felt more loved and taken care of in all her life. It was something she had never dreamed possible—but, with God, Annie realized, all things are possible!

A Letter To Our Readers

Dear Reader:

In order that we might better contribute to your reading enjoyment, we would appreciate your taking a few minutes to respond to the following questions. When completed, please return to the following:

Rebecca Germany, Managing Editor
Heartsong Presents
P.O. Box 719
Uhrichsville, Ohio 44683

1. Did you enjoy reading *Annie's Song?*
   ❏ Very much. I would like to see more books by this author!
   ❏ Moderately
     I would have enjoyed it more if _____

   _____

2. Are you a member of **Heartsong Presents**? ❏Yes ❏No
   If no, where did you purchase this book? _____

   _____

3. What influenced your decision to purchase this book? (Check those that apply.)

   ❏ Cover   ❏ Back cover copy

   ❏ Title   ❏ Friends

   ❏ Publicity   ❏ Other_____

4. How would you rate, on a scale from 1 (poor) to 5 (superior), the cover design? _____

5. On a scale from 1 (poor) to 10 (superior), please rate the following elements.

___Heroine   ___Plot

___Hero   ___Inspirational theme

___Setting   ___Secondary characters

6. What settings would you like to see covered in **Heartsong Presents** books?_____

_____

_____

7. What are some inspirational themes you would like to see treated in future books?_____

_____

_____

8. Would you be interested in reading other **Heartsong Presents** titles?   ❑ Yes   ❑ No

9. Please check your age range:
  ❑ Under 18   ❑ 18-24   ❑ 25-34
  ❑ 35-45   ❑ 46-55   ❑ Over 55

10. How many hours per week do you read? _____

Name _____

Occupation_____

Address _____

City_____ State_____ Zip_____

Cook "Inn" Style

with *The Christian Bed & Breakfast Cookbook*

A companion volume to the popular *Christian Bed & Breakfast Directory*, this tantalizing cookbook includes the "specialties of the house" from bed and breakfast establishments across the United States and Canada. With over 500 pages of recipes such as "Breakfast in a Cookie," "Irish Soda Bread," and "Mississippi Fried Pies" featuring serving suggestions, garnishes, and the history or origin of most recipes, it's more than a bargain at $3.97.

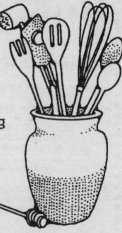

528 pages; paperbound; 5" x 8"

Heart♥ng Presents
Love Stories Are Rated G!

That's for godly, gratifying, and of course, great! If you love a thrilling love story, but don't appreciate the sordidness of some popular paperback romances, **Heartsong Presents** is for you. In fact, **Heartsong Presents** is the *only inspirational romance book club*, the only one featuring love stories where Christian faith is the primary ingredient in a marriage relationship.

Sign up today to receive your first set of four, never before published Christian romances. Send no money now; you will receive a bill with the first shipment. You may cancel at any time without obligation, and if you aren't completely satisfied with any selection, you may return the books for an immediate refund!

Imagine. . .four new romances every four weeks—two historical, two contemporary—with men and women like you who long to meet the one God has chosen as the love of their lives. . .all for the low price of $9.97 postpaid.

To join, simply complete the coupon below and mail to the address provided. **Heartsong Presents** romances are rated G for another reason: They'll arrive *Godspeed!*